BLACK TONGUE

AND OTHER ANOMALIES

RICHARD BEAUCHAMP

D & T
PUBLISHING

For those of you who've shown enough interest in my writings to pick up "Black Tongue and Other Anomalies" you might be wondering what sort of traumatic events this poor soul must've endured to have written about such unpleasantness as what is contained in this collection.

The truth is, my childhood, and my life overall, have been nothing special. I was born and raised in a well-to-do rural midwestern family. I had a good education, a healthy upbringing, and for all intents and purposes, a "normal" life. But what comes back to me time and time again, the one childhood memory that sort of primed my need for story telling was my grandmother, and her spellbinding way of relaying her travels abroad at many a family function.

My grandparents travelled the world for the many decades they were together and have seen and experienced things most people could only dream of. An ardent believer of the afterlife and a studious practitioner of superstition, my grandmother had this way of wrapping you up in every word she spoke as she ruminated on everything from staying in notoriously haunted hotels to being held at gun point in some war-torn part of the middle east as the bus they were riding on was the unfortunate target of a hijacking (just to name a few of her more colorful travels), with my grandfather often nodding in corroboration to her tales.

It was always one of my favorite parts of family dinners, of staying at my grandmother's, hearing her mesmerizing tales of adventure. Looking back, it's hard to decipher how much was factual, and how much was embellishment, but in the end it didn't matter. What mattered was that suspension of belief, that sort of flow state you get when you're cruising along on a good story, not wanting to reach the end, but simply enjoying the journey it's taking you on. My grandmother had exposed me to the addicting properties of storytelling, and ever since, I've been a ravenous consumer of the story in all it's forms, written, visual, auditory, which eventually led to me trying my hand at creating my own stories.

There are countless people I could thank for helping influence my imagination and letting these stories come to fruition.

First and foremost, I want to thank my late grandmother, Willie Storey, aka "Momma Bill" for instilling the seeds of wonder in my brain that would eventually blossom into the imagination responsible for these dark and twisted tales.

A special thanks to my parents, Dale and Stacey, for, you know, giving me that all important spark of life, and doing their best to raise a very strange, very quiet child with an extremely over-active imagination.

My beautiful partner, Sierra, deserves a big thanks for instilling me with confidence and being a foundation of constant support when days of crippling imposter syndrome and anxiety made it nearly impossible for me to get a single word of prose down.

To all the editors from every single anthology, magazine and collection I've submitted to, both the ones who accepted and rejected my stories, especially the ones who took the time to give constructive feedback on my stories, I say thanks.

I guess I have to thank my strange, beautiful home state of Missouri for providing me with the unique rural Americana and it's many colorful denizens that serve as the setting for so many of my stories.

To my readers, the few of you there may be, thank you for letting me take you on these little journeys of my imagination. I hope you enjoyed the ride, and want to come back for more.

Although every page of fiction I've read over my 29 trips around the sun has shaped and influenced my prose and writing style, one book in particular stands out as having pushed me over the edge from being a constant reader to a constant writer. Stephen King's "On Writing" is a text I feel like every budding writer or consumer of fiction should read at least once in their life. Everyone always thinks you need to have a degree in English or take formal writing classes to be any sort of "legit" writer. After reading "On Writing" my *eyes had been thoroughly opened to the fact that anyone with an active imagination and the will power to sit down and dance with the keyboard can be a writer. Masterpieces of fiction can be made by academic scholars and your every day working stiff who sneaks away on his lunch break to work on their guilty pleasure, one word at a time. For that, I want to thank the King. And last but not least, I want to thank Dawn, Tim, and the whole team at D&T Publishing for giving me the chance to publish this collection of stories.*

CONTENTS

Publication History ix
1. Black Tongue 1
2. Castle In the Sky 19
3. Conflagration 39
4. The Golden Shepherd 51
5. Obsidian 58
6. Red Death 70
7. Search and Destroy 85
8. Sons of Luna 99
9. The Chiwaa'e 111
10. The Conversion 125
11. Riene De L'enfer (The Queen of Hell) 134
12. The White Suits 141

Richard Beauchamp 151
About the Editor / Publisher 153

PUBLICATION HISTORY

"Black Tongue" originally appeared in *Negative Space: An Anthology of Survival Horror* published by Dark Peninsula Press.

"Sons of Luna" originally appeared in *Influence of the Moon* published by Pub518.

"Conflagration" originally appeared in *Horror USA: California* by Soteira Press.

"Search And Destroy" originally appeared in *Night Terrors Volume 3* by Scare Street Publishing.

"The White Suits" originally appeared in *Night Terrors Volume 4* by Scare Street Publishing.

"Obsidian" originally appeared in *Night Terrors Volume 5* by Scare Street Publishing.

"Golden Shepherd" originally appeared in audio format on *Episode 4-Cults by The Other Stories*, published by Hawk and Cleaver Audio.

"The Queen of Hell" originally appeared in audio format on *Episode 2-Ghost Ships By The Other Stories*, published by Hawk and Cleaver Audio.

"The Conversion" originally appeared in *Amongst Friends* by Gypsum Sound Tales.

"The Chiwaa'e" originally appeared in *Isolation* by DBND Publishing.

"Red Death" Originally appeared in *Monsters in Spaaaace!* By Dragon's Roost Press.

"Castle In the Sky" has never been published before, and makes it's print debut in this collection.

1

BLACK TONGUE

He was awake in an instant. His body stiffened like a coiled viper, arms shooting out like spring-loaded traps. His hands, made strong by years of bush craft and dealing death, seized a clump of thick black fur. He felt a cold muzzle against his neck, and for a split second he flailed around for a throat, a collarbone, anything he could break or snap, before feeling the tongue on his face and realizing it was Chief.

As soon as he registered the dog, he registered the cold. His body felt like a nearly frozen skeleton, like death reanimated, and he shivered violently. Chief, his pureblood Mastiff, lay next to him for warmth. This was not so much an act of affection as it was of primal instinct—the ultimate goal to keep warm and keep his only pack member alive.

The fire was barely smoldering as he lay awake. He didn't think he would be able to sleep, given last night's phenomena of snapping twigs and Chief's constant low growl. Bronson had owned Chief since he was a pup, and the only time the dog growled was when something bigger and meaner was in the immediate vicinity.

The previous night he had holed up in a small hollow tucked into the side of the ridge. He felt good about having something solid to his back and above him, at least until the strange sounds came. They were the sounds of inquiry, of stealthy investigation by an unseen foe. He thought he would be up all night, listening to those footsteps in the dark—the only other imperative to keep the fire going until dawn. But soon utter exhaustion overtook him, and he fell asleep with his musket within arm's reach.

But the night was just now starting to bleed with sunlight, his surroundings painted in a light blue, and he was awake. Chief was no longer growling, and the perimeter alarms had not gone off. *Warmth. Fire.* The words were mentally spoken like unsaid commands. Then came the matter of food, which they both would need before continuing their journey.

He roused himself and left the musket by the fire pit, taking only his two-shot flintlock pistol and bone dagger, making sure both hammers on the flintlock weren't frozen in place. He exited the hollow.

"Chief, come," he said, stepping around the edge of the cove and up the rocky incline. Large fir trees jutted up into the heavens, standing like silent sentries, occasionally offering him the gift of a fallen branch. The bark was still thick with resin that ignited like kerosene. Ahead, Chief bounded off with thick snuffling noises as the canine sniffed out some unidentified scent.

Normally he would let the dog run off and pick up the scent. Chief's snout was a prodigal tracker of deer and hare, but he couldn't risk the dog going out of his line of sight. According to the terrified villagers who'd hired him, every single victim had disappeared alone, either off in the forest hunting or coming home late from the logging mill. He needed the dog's protection and tracking skills more than he needed fresh meat.

They walked for a few minutes when Bronson came to a pine tree. The branches were not too overladen with snow. He placed the knife against one branch, used the pistol handle as a club, and clubbed off one of the thinner branches with three strikes. The sharp scent of pine resin filled his nose. Such a clean, blessed smell. It was the smell that always preceded fire.

He chopped off a few more branches and peeled off bits of the bark from around the base of the tree, then slipped them into his pocket. They would be useful for kindling. Bronson was so engrossed in the activity that he didn't notice Chief's absence. Then he heard the bassoon roar of barking in the distance.

"Chief!" he called out, stuffing a few more pieces of kindling into his pocket. He listened to the barking, but the snow sometimes messed with the acoustics. He realized the barking was coming off to his left, down a slender ridge. He ran in that direction, old boots slipping on the frozen earth. He rounded one of the snow-covered pine trees and came upon Chief.

Surrounded by snow-covered conifers stood a sheared pine tree. The branches had been stripped off and the base was blackened and scorched, as if sundered by lightning. Lashed to the tree and using its own muscles and sinews as bindings, was the corpse of an adult stag. Its ribcage had been flayed open. The guts sat at the base of the tree, still steaming in the cold. One hoof twitched sporadically.

"Chief! Heel!" he yelled, but his voice held no conviction. He stared at the mutilated corpse, his rational mind desperately trying to tell him a cougar could do this. So far all the disappearances in the isolated logging camp had the mark of a big mama cougar. Not anymore.

He had once been paid a half pound in gold to find a missing company of miners in the eastern part of Colorado. He mainly took the job to confirm their deaths so their families could lay claim to their collected ore. He eventually found what was left of two of the bodies, tucked way up in an ancient hackberry tree. Chief had picked up the cougar's scent and cornered the huge feline as it was making its way up an aspen tree, an effort that won the dog a three-lined scar across his muzzle. Bronson dispatched it with a single musket shot and it fell howling and bleeding from the tree. He never found the other three men.

But from his experience, no cougar could do this to a stag. Not even close. It looked like the villagers had a more dangerous predator in their midst.

He glanced around and saw the forest was completely barren. Fear tightened his bladder and shriveled his scrotum and made him even more aware of the bitter cold, and he longed for the meager shelter and fire he had found in the night.

He grabbed the dog by the thick scruff, dragging the eighty-pound animal away from the carcass. Chief finally relented, and ran off towards the cove, where the safe scents of burned wood and the man's oiled steel fire breather lay.

Bronson followed the dog back to the hollow where a few charred chunks of pine trunk still smoldered. His right hand was sticky with resin, and he prayed whatever it was in these isolated woods that had mutilated the stag would not choose this moment to attack, where a misfire with his flintlock was sure to happen.

But he was granted a small blessing in getting to camp safely with the kindling. Dropping to his knees, his hands shaking from adrenaline and cold, he stooped over the ash pit, roughing up the twigs from his pocket and chopping the bark up with his knife. Then he fumbled around in his leather satchel for the flint and jagged piece of Union-issued steel from a bayonet. Sparks jumped eagerly from the bayonet, and he willed their embers to find the flammable resin and give him the gift of warmth with a few breaths to stoke it.

With the kindling lit, he carefully added in more bark until it was blazing. He could feel the frozen snot in his beard melting and his nose running and his face stinging with heat, and he was thankful for all of it. Both he and the dog huddled around the blaze, and the man known as Bronson Calloway ruminated on his circumstances, forcing himself to admit they could become dire at the smallest misstep.

AFTER PREPARING a meal of hard tack and salted pork, half of which went to the dog, he melted some snow and made coffee while Chief lapped up water from a puddle near the fire. He pulled out the rough map given by one of the village's logging men and consulted it. The map was written in French. Many of the territory names he had translated to English.

Judging from the map, he was approximately twenty miles from where he had departed, a French logging camp called *Jardin Des Dieux*. From there, he had taken several trails cleared by lumberjacks and boarded a hand operated cart down the most shoddily built railroad he had ever seen. While he traveled, he began to see the wildlands of untamed rough country. He figured that by now he must have crossed over into the Canadian territories. But the Frenchmen promised him payment in American dollars regardless of where his hunt concluded.

He knew he was somewhere along the base of the Gallatin Range, and the two circles indicated his areas of interest were still a few miles north. He would continue following the ridge, while looking for any signs of predator activity. He would also keep a look out for signs of natives, as a man named Louis Lamont—head of the Lamont logging mill outside the village—had warned him about. Bronson's French wasn't the best, but from what he could gather, Louis told him about the tribes of Lakota and Cheyenne who were cut off from their home tribes during Custer's incursion of the Montana territories. They sometimes came upon the logging villages, terrorizing the loggers and attacking the Frenchmen, who they called *wasichus,* out of crazed grief for having their homes so brutally taken from them.

Bronson prayed that the surly French logger was wrong about that. He had heard stories from those of the 7th battalion, of the ruthlessness of the Cheyenne, how they could materialize from the ground and how you'd have an arrow or hatchet stuck in you before you knew what was happening. The lone hunter knew if he came upon a tribe, especially some isolated raiding party, he would be tortured and killed. Castration, scalping and disembowelment were common rituals. In that matter, he would shove the big bore flintlock in his mouth before they could capture him.

His thoughts came back to the stag. The rib cage had been pried open, an act that would require dexterous hands. A bear perhaps could do such damage. But the big Kodiaks that ventured this far north were smelly, noisy creatures, and other than the occasional sounds of stealthy locomotion, the forest had been dead silent.

He left his makeshift camp while the sun was still rising, taking a torch with him so that he may have some burnable charcoal for later. He went along the side of the mountain, slowly zigzagging up as he found the path of least resistance ascending the slope. Louis had told him about a spot on the other side of Grey's Peak where a company of his men set up a new mill. They had left three weeks ago, but because of the increasing number of disappearances, no one dared seek them out.

Bronson had been walking for around four hours when he descended a ridge and came upon the remains of a primitive base camp. Two large pine trees lay unprocessed next to cleanly cut stumps, along with the ashy remains of a small fire and two canvas tents. He could see a boot sticking out from the bottom of the tent. Chief had already approached the camp and was sniffing around the other tent.

"Hello? Bonjour?" Bronson's rough voice called out. No response, not that he was expecting any. Cautiously, he approached the camp, his flintlock at his side, the musket unslung and ready to fire. His eyes tried to take in everything, searching for movement or anomalies in the scenery.

The camp was tucked between two ridge walls where a piece of rock jutted out in the middle, creating a somewhat level surface for them to set up shop. He saw a row of mature ponderosa pines on either side, the size of which were rare even out here in the deep range. He could see why they chose this spot.

With the barrel of his musket, he Opened one tent flap and saw that the boot belonged to a pair of legs which did not have an upper body. From the waist up was nothing but a messy stump of frozen innards and the gleaming white nub of spine. Tatters of browned, dried flesh and flannel shreds lay poking up from blood-stained trousers. Next to the legs was a blood-stained bundle of wool blankets, a few double-handled saws, a portable stove, and a half empty glass bottle filled with amber fluid. He picked the bottle up, uncorked it, smelled. Whiskey.

He went over to the other tent where Chief stood guard. Inside he found the corpse of a man lying down on his makeshift bed. The man had a flintlock pistol, similar to his own, held in both hands, the barrel half in his mouth. Long black hair that floated like a bushy aurora around the head was caked with frozen blood. The white canvas directly behind him was crusted with frozen blood and brain matter, a few shards of skull stuck to the gore. Also there was a journal, two large splitting axes, and a cloth sack containing cured pork and some beef tallow that was frozen solid. A can of kerosene and two smashed lanterns were in another corner. He grabbed the journal and exited the tent.

From this elevation he could see a vast panorama of the sprawling valley below, and in the distance were dark clouds sliding over the tops of distant peaks. His stomach dropped to his knees as he realized more snow was coming. Three hundred and fifty dollars…that was his pay for eliminating the man (or men) responsible for snatching away the people of *Jardin Des Dieux*. But so far all he found was inexplicable violence and madness. A blizzard was rolling in from the east, and he was some thirty miles from the nearest hint of civilization.

You can turn back now. Wouldn't be the first time you've called off a hunt. You're getting too old for this kind of hogwash.

But he cast off the voice, the voice of an old frail man, the voice of entropy weakening his resolve. He needed that money. He had debts to pay and a woman with child in her belly that needed providing for, and this was all he knew. He decided then to make camp here tonight. He had slept among dead men before.

Working quickly, he investigated the immediate perimeter of the camp, not finding the missing half of body that belonged to the legs in the first tent, but finding two nearly processed logs, and making a mental note to come back here with one of the splitting axes to gather firewood. He had a feeling he'd need as much wood as he could get tonight.

He then went about dragging the corpses out of their tents, trying to handle the remains with respect while also working fast to beat the descending sun. He moved the bodies down the ridge, then chose the tent which had the severed legs in it since it had the least amount of blood inside. He cut apart the tent the man had killed himself in, and used the few torn sheets of canvas to patch up the rips on the other tent.

As he worked, he made a mental game plan. He would stay here tonight, waiting out the blizzard. Come first light, he would head out regardless of the weather and continue north. He figured if something nearby was stalking him, he would find its tracks and follow them back to its den and end this once and for all.

By the time he was done setting up camp, twilight was already injecting darkness across the surrounding landscape. Soon after, the clouds came. They were thick and heavy, as were the snowflakes that bled from their ethereal bellies. He got the fire burning big and bright, using the ambient lighting to set up wire-triggered alarms across the perimeter surrounding his camp.

With that done, he helped himself to some of the whiskey, then cracked open the journal. The writing was hard to decipher in places, and he found himself huddled by the fire rereading passages over and over, trying to recall as many French words as he could from his brief time working in Alberta as a trapper and fur trader. From what he could make out, the man who killed himself, Claude, expressed doubt at setting up a new mill here. Something about the streams tasting fowl and the wildlife behaving strangely.

A few pages in, he read what sounded like incoherent nonsense.

John is missing, John is missing. The trees speak, and know me. They tell me my wife is out here. They have her. My god they have her... Leonard is here but not here. He is possessed... He is... with them. The black tongue. He's tried to kill me. We shouldn't be here.

He flipped back a few pages, wondering if perhaps he had missed something. He came to a page marked February 8th, 1869. Two weeks ago.

Mountain Shaman with a Lakota family, inbred it appears, came upon us today. Thought they would attack but they were running. Claude knows some Lakota. Family says that we can't stay here. They had done something wrong, something they couldn't stop. They said they were running from the speaker of the black tongue, and that the whole countryside was now corrupt with its influence. Claude couldn't understand it all, but they took off before he could ask further.

He drank more of the whiskey to calm his nerves and focused again on the journal. He reread the rambling bits, wondering if he had mistranslated some of the words. Snow hissed as it fell into the fire, which, despite the logs and a few drops of kerosene, was low and always on the verge of extinguishing.

Chief suddenly jumped up and started growling. Bronson got to his feet, his head reeling slightly from the whiskey, and peered into the snowstorm. Beyond the fire, everything was a white blur. Chief then exited the tent and started barking outside.

"Chief, heel!" he said, trying to get the dog to stop so he could listen. He exited the dwelling and noticed that Chief faced away from the fire, head down, jowls quivering as his teeth gnashed at the air, breath coming out in white plumes. After more commands, the dog quit barking, instead issuing a thunderous rumbling deep in his throat that would cause even a starving alpha wolf to reconsider its options.

Yet over the deep throaty growl, Bronson heard the unmistakable clatter of his wire traps. Then he heard a dragging sound that grew louder. Something coming toward them, something utterly unphased by the warning vocalizations of the huge snarling beast at his side. This fact alone made Bronson stumble back and drop the whiskey bottle as he grabbed the flintlock pistol sitting atop his caribou blanket in the tent.

"Stop! Or I'll shoot!" he said, as a shape materialized out of the whirling flecks of white. *"Arret!"* he called out in French. But the figure, which carried itself forward with jerky, clumsy locomotion, did not respond to either language. Bronson saw it was too small to be a man. Then he noticed several other smaller shapes alongside it.

Bronson cocked the first hammer on the pistol. He took aim at the larger figure, his hand wavering slightly, and he took his other hand and steadied the arm. He fired, a report that thundered briefly across the forest before being swallowed by the snow. The shape twitched, a definite hit, but did not stop coming. Heart pounding, breath exploding from him, he cocked the other hammer and shot again. This time he saw the snow-covered ground just ahead of the figure explode in a plume of white. None of the approaching shapes hesitated in the slightest.

Bronson was about to turn and reach for his musket when Chief took off, bounding into the white blur like a gray arrow launched from an unseen bow. He called after the dog, but it was no use. The beast exploded into the night, a blurred form that met the approaching specters head on. There was a snarl as Chief's massive jaws locked onto something, his head ripping back and forth before he slung something from his jaws, where it landed a few feet from the fire.

Bronson saw it was a hare, but not a freshly killed one. Half the fur was missing, the skin gray and blackened in some spots, the bowels gone, the eyes cloudy raisins. It looked to have been dead for at least a week. Next to it was the top half of the body from the campsite.

The upper torso of the Frenchman walked on his hands through the snow. He had on the tatters of a wool jacket, the exposed skin almost as white as the snow. Bronson could see the fist-sized hole in the man's chest where he had shot him, but no blood oozed from the wound. The truncated man had a large brown beard similar to Bronson's, with several small bones braided into it, like that of the Indian war chiefs and their battle dress. One eye was clouded over and sunken deep into its socket, the other gone, the strand of its optic nerve dangling from a pulpy cavern. His skull was missing from the brow up.

The dead man stopped a few feet from the fire, his face expressionless, head pointed toward Bronson. Behind the man stood a row of animals, a few deer, one cougar cub, and three snow hares. By the light of the fire, Bronson could make out the various stages of decomposition, with exposed rib cages, huge gaping bloodless wounds, all missing parts of their skulls. Bronson had seen some truly horrible things during the war, like what an artillery barrage could do to human bodies, or what a blunderbuss blast at close range could do to a skull. But this abhorrent display of absurdity robbed him of thought or speech.

He meant to grab his musket, but he could only stand there. He was vaguely aware that Chief was at his side. The dog charged at an animal on the outside right of the row, one of the deer, but the creature seemed unaware of the jaws ripping away huge swathes of its flesh. Chief bit down on one of its legs and ripped it away. The deer stumbled, but did not fall. Then there was a choking sound from Chief, and the dog began to shake its head wildly, stumbling off through the snow.

"*Tu,*" the dead man said. The word came out as a papery rasp, produced by atrophied vocal cords that hung in the air like a poisoned cloud. After a moment, it spoke again. "*Vas mourir ici.*" Then it threw itself on the fire, as did the animated entourage of decrepit forest animals. Foul smoke bellowed out from the smothered flames as the corpses burned, rapidly putrefying as the glowing coals of the nearly extinguished fire cooked their bodies, as if the corpses themselves had been coated in kerosene.

You will die here.

He was almost positive that's what the animated corpse said to him.

The night dimmed into a white wave of nothing as the fire went out, the smoldering corpses letting out an odor so thick and putrid that it caused Bronson to heave up his modest dinner of jerky and whiskey. With the contents of his stomach voided, he stumbled past the foul smoke towards the direction he had seen his beloved canine run.

"Chief! Come!" he called into the white void, but he did not hear or see the dog. He kept walking, a walk that turned into a shambling run as panic set in. Then he stopped, listening. He thought he heard something—a thin, pathetic whimpering off to his right. He bolted in that direction, heart pounding.

He nearly stumbled over Chief's snow-covered body. Half of a hare's corpse lay by his head, the body oozing a foul black ichor that pooled in the snow. A small lake of brown and yellow vomit sunk into the snow next to Chief's head, and Bronson could see bits of bone and fur in the expulsion.

"Come on boy, get up," he said, putting his hands underneath the heavy dog to try and get him to his feet. For a moment the mastiff stood, but the legs trembled and buckled. The dog let out a thick grunt as it tried to vomit once more. Whatever insidious energy had animated the corpses had also poisoned the vessels in which it piloted, and his dog had consumed the poison.

When it was clear that Chief couldn't move, Bronson picked the dog up, carrying him over his shoulder the way the Union had taught him to carry his fallen brothers in war. The dog whined, a high, heart-wrenching sound in his throat that almost caused Bronson to be sick as well. But he wouldn't allow himself. Both of them couldn't be sick, whimpering messes.

Arms aching and back screaming, he carried the dog all the way back to camp. He set Chief down outside the tent. The smoke from the fire was a physical entity now, strong enough to push him away every time he tried to grab a smoldering stick or log for a new fire. So instead he melted snow with the heat of his hands, cupping the stinging water and trying to bring it to Chief's muzzle. But the dog refused to drink; nor did he even sniff at the fat-covered pork he usually ate so ravenously.

There was nothing he could do except wait through the night to see if the dog would improve. He retreated into his tent, shivering as the temperature dropped. He wanted fire, but the snow had covered everything, and the latest events had shocked his mind deeply. He was not a man of faith or of paranormal belief. But what he had just witnessed forced him to accept tales and possibilities he had always scoffed at with the comfort of cold logic.

He finished the whiskey, savoring the brief and numbing warmth. After some time, he went to check on Chief. But the dog was cold and rigid to the touch. The great barrel chest did not move. No steam puffed from his snout.

Bronson got on his knees next to the dog, putting his head against its chest. He wanted to hold Chief and grieve over this sudden and unexpected tragedy. But the bitter cold forced him back into his shelter. He thought he would be up all night, tortured by this horrible turn of events. Instead, as a sort of primal defense mechanism, his mind shut down, and he fell into the merciful oblivion of sleep.

WHEN HE AWOKE, Chief was gone. He spotted a trail leading from his tent into the woods, heading west. He knelt down, examined the shallow valley carved into the snow, and found a few course hairs from Chief's coat. It looked like something had come in from the abyssal night and dragged the heavy dog through the snow, out into God knows where, without waking Bronson.

For several minutes, he just screamed. He screamed until his throat burned and his vision swam with black motes. He screamed his sanity away. The combined grief of losing Chief and the utter absurdity of the night's events had broken his once rugged resolve. After that brief episode of catharsis, he numbly went about packing his things. He loaded the flintlock and double checked the charge in his musket to see that it was still good. He slung this around his shoulder, tucked the pistol into his fur coat, and grabbed the can of kerosene, putting it in his rucksack.

Then he began to walk, slowly and with resignation. He had dealt death to countless beings, both human and animal over his lifetime. And he would deal it now, or be the recipient of it. That dichotomy simplified things, and helped him stay on the path, to push his grieving, sore body across the hellish tundra.

As he walked, he noticed various structures comprised of hide and bone that hung from the ponderosas. They were wreaths constructed of human ribcages and tanned skin. He saw trees that had withered and died, collapsing into the snow with pulpy, hollowed-out innards.

Lucifer himself resides in these woods, and we are his playthings. There is no escape. Other than death.

That page of the journal floated up to him, no longer sounding like insane ramblings but a matter of fact. He was heading toward the peak of the mountain, the terrain getting steeper the further he went. In the distance, he could see the black maw of a cave tucked into the side far up near the peak. The trail, which was now clearly marked by a smear of dark violet and more dog hair, seemed to lead there.

He proceeded another fifty arduous yards before two shapes burst out of the snow piled around the trees. They were foxes, and despite the rotten tendons and damaged vessels that this unknown force occupied, they still moved with agile speed. One leaped out and clamped onto Bronson's calf, the other made a suicidal sprint forward, trying to climb up his back, tearing at the pack. Bronson whirled and thrashed, knocking the fox from his back, but the one on his leg held fast, its small fangs sinking deep into his leg.

He cried out in pain, then snarled with rage as he took one large hand, seizing the pointy snout and prying up. He clamped the creature's bottom jaw with his left hand. Up close he could see the mangy fur, the gaping hole in the abdomen where no organs remained, and knew he was dealing with Hell's minions, not rabid predators. He pulled as hard as he could, and a great ripping sound filled the mountain air as he tore the corpse in two, dropping the twitching halves at his sides. The other fox nipped at his ankles, and he raised one heavy snow-crusted boot and brought it down, the skull caving in like an egg shell.

"Is that all you got!" he tried to yell, his voice coming out as a hoarse croak. He kept going, his pistol out now, the knife in his other hand. He forced his aching skeleton forward despite the searing heat in his calf. He felt himself transforming into something no longer man. He was reverting into something more animal, that operated purely on rage and grief.

He started to jog. The cave opening grew larger and loomed like the toothless mouth of some great leviathan. He could see more macabre decorations lining the mouth of the cave, and sigils painted in blood against the high rock walls.

He was looking at the symbols, realizing there was something vaguely native about them, like cave paintings but much more intricate. Then he heard it—the low rumble of the mastiff.

"Chief?" he called out.

From the mouth of the cave, a furry head appeared. The eyes were clouded over, and one of Chief's jowls had been ripped off, the left side of his face now a permanent snarl as his large yellowed teeth shone. At the sight of Bronson, there was the briefest flicker of recognition, of longing, before the creature let out a rusty bark, and charged.

"Chief," he said again, his voice defeated, hollow. But the huge dog didn't recognize him anymore. It sprang forward, paws kicking up plumes of snow. Bronson quickly tucked away his pistol and swung the musket around, carefully putting the knife in the front pocket of his coat. He trailed the dog with the barrel of the gun, lining up the shot, until he was no more than ten feet away. Chief lunged, and Bronson anticipated the move, as it was a trademark of Chief's hunting method. He pulled the trigger.

The dog became lost in a blur of fire and smoke as Bronson was thrown off his feet, the dog hurtling into him. They tumbled in the snow, and he felt the dog's teeth lock onto his forearm. He tried to buck and thrash, but the heavy dog had him pinned down.

He rocked to one side, forcing his mauled arm up to keep Chief from biting at his jugular, and he reached inside his coat for the knife. In an instant, the knife was out, and he plunged it into the dog's broad side to no effect. He nearly dropped the knife in agony as he heard a crunch. The bone in his forearm broke with a hot cleaving force.

He fought through the pain, raised the knife up and brought it down hard on Chief's skull. The blade stuck a few inches into the beast's head. He pushed down with all his might. There was a grinding, splitting noise as he sunk the knife deeper into the skull, until finally Chief's jaws went slack, the body limp.

He shoved the dog off of him with his good hand, and saw the caved in section of chest cavity where the musket ball had hit. He brushed off the innards of his pet, left the musket behind and proceeded into the mouth of the cave. He would mourn for his friend later.

It was dark in the cave, and he remembered the small torch he had kept stashed in his bag. Clumsily, he shrugged off the bag, took out the charred stick wrapped in a fat-soaked rag, and then dug around for the small pack of matches he had found at the camp site. He could still move his fingers on the broken arm, even though it hung at a crooked angle from the elbow, and he gingerly held the striking surface in the bloody fingers, striking the match with his other hand.

After a few tries, he got the match ignited and held it to the torch. He shrugged his bag back on, keeping the flintlock tucked into his coat, where he could easily drop the torch and grab it if he had too. He entered the cave.

THE CAVE DESCENDED IN A WINDING, ever narrowing passageway covered with symbols and pictures of unidentifiable beasts. The farther in he went, the stronger the smell of death and decay became. Twice he came upon more creatures, a wolf that charged before it saw the fire, then retreated past him, sprinting towards the exit. The same thing happened with a mountain lion, except this one ran further back into the cave, hissing as it retreated. He realized they were afraid of the fire.

Eventually he came to a spot that opened up into a large cavern. By the meager glow of the torch he saw someone sitting in the far corner, muttering something that sounded like bastardized Lakota. He swung the torch around and saw mountain creatures huddled against the walls. They surrounded the man who sat cross-legged on a throne made of various skeletons and hides. Spread out before him were four clay tablets, with script and symbols.

The man had a vicious scar running across one side of his face, going across the eye, which was scarred over and white. The other eye was rolled up, moving underneath the half-raised lid. He was muttering incessantly, perhaps an incantation or prayer. He had several bone piercings and tribal scarring along his naked body. Black tendrils that looked like veins had burst through the skin at many points, disappearing into the mountain through cracks in the ground. These black veins pulsed, as if the mountain itself had a beating heart. Something moved off to Bronson's right, and he whirled around and saw a mangled corpse of a disemboweled white man in logging clothes bound to the wall.

"Stop," the white man said in lilting English. "The blood ritual has not been finished. Destroying us will only—"

Bronson didn't want to hear any more. He set the torch to the man's shirt.

A rusted, grating scream issued from the thing as the shirt caught fire, the matted beard quickly becoming engulfed. The man fell to the ground as his netting of sinew and muscle lit up. He collapsed into a burning heap.

Bronson shrugged off his bag and put the handle of the torch in his teeth. He groped around until his hand found the jar of kerosene. He took it out, braced the bottom against the floor and turned the lid with his good hand. The crisp tang of kerosene was a clean odor compared to the foul decay that filled the cave. At some point, the muttering man, the orchestrator of this whole macabre show, must have understood what Bronson meant to do.

He heard scurrying as the animals charged, but he had already tossed the kerosene out onto the rooted man, who may have at one time been a shaman, a father, a war lord, something more human than he was now. Bronson tossed the torch into the man's lap where the fluid puddled, and with a low *whoomph*, the man was up in flames. A split second later the cougar had tackled him, saber teeth mauling his back. He didn't try to fight. He landed on his broken arm and the pain was so intense that he almost blacked out.

But then the massive beast was off his back, and there was a sizzling sound. The animals had jumped on the man, trying to smother the fire. But the kerosene was too potent; the lumberjacks must have known where to get the high quality kind, for the blaze burned strong, and that horrible acrid smoke filled the cave.

The fur and dried skin of the dead animals burned like kindling, only serving to feed the flames. The black roots embedded into the burning man's flesh ripped away and flailed like blazing snakes, retreating back into the cracks with hissing pops.

Soon it became hard to breathe, and Bronson struggled to his feet.

He wanted to lay there and die. But then he remembered what he had left behind, the fact he was going to be a father. He felt an imperative need to escape, not for his own safety, but so that his child may have a father to protect him or her in this world, where such ghastly things existed.

As he scrambled out of the cave, his eyes fell upon something—the four stone tablets written in that strange language. The black tongue. Not knowing why, he grabbed the stone tablets and stuffed them into his pack, then exited the cave.

He collapsed on the ground, foul smoke billowing out from behind him. He looked around, amazed at the conflagration before him. The whole forest crawling up the side of the mountain was beginning to burn, trees randomly bursting into flames. Great clouds of steam and smoke obscured his view of the valley as snow melted and met fire.

He forced himself to get up and walked over to Chief's corpse, staring down at the animal who'd had his back on countless occasions. The animal he'd raised from a delicate, mewling puppy, to a fierce but loyal companion.

Bronson reached over and felt the comforting coat, that familiar rough fur, running his fingers through it like he used to do when Chief was just a pup. His vision blurred as tears froze to his cheeks. He wanted to lie down next to his traveling companion, to fall asleep next to that thick fur coat while the fire raged.

But he knew he couldn't. He had to survive. He would bury Chief like he had his other friends in war, then carry on the fight. Because there was great evil in this world, he understood now, and the righteous fire that surrounded him had yet to touch its cleansing flames to all those other abominations.

2

CASTLE IN THE SKY

"Easy, Parker, easssy," came Anna's voice through the headset. Parker looked up, the surface looming closer like a massive azure sheet. From what he could tell, the skies were clear, which was a good sign. He'd begun his excruciatingly slow ascent some three hours ago from substation Alpha, located two miles below, his advanced diving suit helping to accelerate the depressurizing process. As the surface grew closer, he could see his target some fifty feet away, a large oblong shadow, the hull cutting ten feet into the water. A military research vessel according to the substation's radar reading. The distress beacon on the ship had still been pinging all this time, even though the crew were no doubt dead.

"ETA three minutes until contact. How's my nitrogen level looking?" Parker asked, trying to hide the shake in his voice. It was only his third time to the surface, he was the first of a generation born below water, and to him the surface was an almost mythical place.

"You're fine, P. N-O level stable," Anna's reassuring voice told him. He longed to see the sky, to look at the sun, to be able to look up and not see miles of dark oppressive water sitting above him. But he knew he couldn't afford to sightsee. His mission was simple, get aboard, take stock of supplies, have alpha team send up SAM-V if there was anything worth taking, and get the fuck out of there before the floaters came.

His gloved hands touched the rusted metal of the hull. He worked his way along the side until he found the rungs he was looking for.

"Breaching the surface. You'll be hearing from me shortly," Parker said, and with his heart hammering in his chest, climbed aboard.

ACCORDING to the faded lettering on the side, the ship was called the HMS Burke. Parker relayed this to the substation comms.

"That's a British naval frigate. Should be some good stuff on there. I'll go ahead and send up SAM," said Randy, the remaining engineer who worked and maintained the semi-autonomous marine vehicle, or SAM as they called it. Parker climbed up the gun metal gray hull until he was on the front deck. On one side was the large command tower and bridge, where strange looking equipment that looked totally alien to Parker cast long shadows on the deck. He swayed slightly as the ship rocked with the waves. He took a few steps towards a door marked GALLEY ACCESS/CREWS QUARTERS/STORAGE. He pointed his helmet at it so Anna could see through his mounted camera.

"That's it. According to the ship schematics all the goods should be below deck. Jesus this is great. I bet there's enough food up there to last us months," she said excitedly. Parker headed down, opening the heavy metal door and gasping at the sight before him. Three corpses were strewn about the narrow stairwell, dried gore painting the walls. Their navy uniforms moldered and clung to their exploded bodies. "Don't pay attention to them, just keep going," Anna said, Parker knowing she picked up his spike in vitals. He took a deep breath and continued below deck.

Down below he found more corpses lying about the narrow corridors, doing his best to ignore them as he searched for supply crates. He followed Anna's directions, going left, then right, until he came upon a large area with several tables and a dozen corpses, their internal matter splattered across the walls as if they'd all swallowed pipe bombs. He swallowed back his gorge, afraid he was going to puke in his suit.

"Focus, Parker. Go to the rear. You should see some crates labelled for food," Anna said. Parker did so, going towards a back kitchen area, eventually finding several crates labelled MRE's and PERISHABLES. Anna directed him to start hauling the MRE crates topside for extraction. They were heavy, and his progress was slow.

"Wait, wait, it's gonna take all fuckin day for him to get those crates loaded up," Randy said. "There should be a lift mechanism for the lifeboats, if you can turn the engines on, you should be able to fill one of the lifeboats with goods and lower it into the water, then just toss it into the sub and be done with it." Parker dropped the first of the heavy boxes and was directed by Anna to leave and go across the ship, towards the bridge. He ran, beginning to feel incredibly exposed under the deceptively empty skies. After climbing several sets of stairs and entering through a shattered window—all the windows were broken out—he came across a large room that overlooked the whole ship, with consoles and another corpse, this one in a white uniform with distinguished lapels and badges. Parker noticed the man had a gun in his hand, his corpse not imploded like the others. Just a single head wound. He put the pieces together in his mind.

Randy talked him through the sequence to fire up the engines.

"You sure they will even start? It's been twenty years, Ran," Anna said,

"Oh they'll fire. Those babies are diesel behemoths, meant to run in a fuckin nuclear apocalypse if they had too." Randy was right. After turning a few switches and several knobs, Parker felt vibration beneath his feet as the whole ship hummed to life. Lights flicked on, and he saw a piece of paper on the control console, the withered hand of the captain holding it in place. Knowing Anna could see his movements, he looked away as he did this, tucking the piece of paper into one of his storage compartments.

"Alright, see those eight orange buttons? Hit all of them, those are the skiff lifts," Randy said, and Parker did so. He saw the platforms with the orange lifeboats lower on all sides of the ship. "Alright, now all you gotta do is take the crates and walk across the mess hall to the outside deck, lifeboat 4A should be right next to the hull door." Parker left the captain's bridge and ran back the way he came, back down into the galley. By the time he got there he was sweating and exhausted, the heavy pressurization suit not meant for that kind of movement.

He began to carry the crates across the hall, through the open porthole door and into the lifeboat that hung suspended from a winch system. Once he'd gotten four crates in, he went for the perishables.

"Don't bother with those, they're probably rotten," Anna said.

"Hey kid, mind doing me a favor?" Randy said. "Check around those shelves in the kitchen, look for a glass bottle with some kind of amber liquid in it."

"Seriously, Randy? I'm not putting my son's life in danger just so you can get some fucking booze," Anna said, but Parker was already on it. He wanted to prove his worth to the team, and he'd get everything they asked for. *No more treating me like a kid after this mission*, he thought smugly. He quickly ransacked the shelves until he found two dark glass bottles with labels on them that had strange names.

"Cabernet! Nice! Good work Parker," Randy said jubilantly. He could hear his mother sighing over the headset.

"Alright. Now, let's see if we can find some medical supplies. Go to —" Anna began before another voice chimed in. It was Susanna. She was the one in charge of keeping track of the EMF visualizer, which could detect abnormalities in the earth's magnetic field from hundreds of miles away.

"No time, looks like we got a portal forming three miles due east of the ship's position. Shit, the engines turning on must have attracted them. Parker, get the hell out of there now," she said.

"But what about the supplies? We're running low, we can't—" Randy began, before his mother cut the technician off.

"Screw the fucking supplies, Parker, get on that sub!" his mother nearly screamed. Parker ran outside, dropping the wine in the boat and hitting the emergency release switch. He peered over the hull as the boat dropped down into the water, looking for the yellow body of SAM to appear. It was nowhere in sight.

"Sub is still fifty meters down and rising. I'm hurrying," Randy said, his voice tight with concentration. Parker's comms erupted in chatter as the members struggled to figure out what to do. He ignored all of them, instead running down to the bow and looking up to the sky. He'd never seen a floater before, and was still entirely unsure of how truthful his mother had been about the supposedly god-like creatures. He stared up into the clear blue sky, where he saw the most beautiful thing. He felt his body go slack and his pupils dilate as he looked up at the swirling purple vortex in the sky.

He watched the star dust swirl hypnotically, felt himself growing intoxicated like he'd just taken a swig of Randy's station shine. Then he felt the atmosphere change, even through his suit. For a split second the world felt just as devoid of oxygen as it did below water, and then came the boom. Though tinny and distorted through his suit's exterior microphone, he could feel it, the shockwave that followed the sonic boom. He was thrown back some fifteen feet, suit bouncing off the wall and falling on the walkway, the ship rocking violently.

When he regained his composure, he looked up, confused, as the sky was no longer there. He stretched his head back, and where there was once sky was now a mottled brown texture that seemed to ripple and quiver in a million different spots. The huge insect like carapace stretched for miles, blotting out sun and clouds. Long rope-like appendages dropped from this massive corporeal vessel, and at their ends were shimmering purple lights that drew in Parker's eyes no matter how hard he fought to look away. *The death lights.* He'd heard about these, even seen them from underwater as they floated around in the sub, looking for places to scavenge. But he'd never seen where those lights came from.

He was faintly aware of his mother screaming at him through the comms channel, but she was far away somewhere. The only thing that mattered was the purple light. Even as he felt his skin begin to boil, his insides beginning to liquify and a white hot agony assaulting him on a molecular level, the light was all that mattered. It was so beautiful, it was divine. Then his eyeballs ruptured in their sockets, and it was only then that he became fully aware of the pain.

HER HUSBAND HAD GONE the same way. What she heard through the comms was almost identical to Howard's demise. Moans of awe, wonder, followed by shrieks of pain, before the liquid squelching of a human body imploding coated the microphone. She slammed a fist against the controls and stood up, almost hitting her head on the roof. Despite living down here for over twenty years, she still sometimes forgot just how cramped her confines were. She walked out of external communications bay three and walked across the walkway to the main hub. She stared through the glass walls of the walkway, watching as a huge manta ray swam lazily past. She knew not to stare too long through the glass. They'd had several members of their crew go crazy over the years from claustrophobia and generalized anxiety disorders. Reminding herself of the world she could no longer inhabit didn't help matters.

Randy and Susanna were already in the HUB, pained looks on their faces.

"Anna...Hey—" Susanna began but Anna hushed her with a hand up.

"Save your condolences. I don't wanna fucking hear it," she said, tears brimming in her eyes. She yanked the flask from Randy's hands, drank deeply of the foul moonshine he brewed in the agra-chamber using corn and filtered sea water. It tasted like nail polish, but the numbing effect was instant. "We need to fucking kill those things. Or one of them, at least. I can die happy knowing we took one of those big bastards out," she said. The crew was silent for a moment.

"Anna, you know that's not possible. If all the world's armies combined couldn't do it, well... what makes you think—"

"Those armies were bound by international protocol. Remember E-day? When President Jennings authorized the nukes? We took one out, then. I know we did; I saw its fucking carcass fall into the ocean. The impact was so massive it caused a tidal wave. After that, nuclear attacks were condemned. Fucking shame." Her voice was acidic at the memory. It had been two weeks since the creatures had first travelled through the worm holes mankind was using to travel across the stars when the POTUS, finally understanding these incredible entities were hostile, had sent four thermonuclear warheads into the belly of one leviathan that floated a few miles off the coast of Boston. The powers that be had no idea those portals would attract the interdimensional beings to their neck of the woods. Had no idea they even existed. But still she couldn't help harbor contempt for IUT, or Intra-Universal Transport, the private company who funded the research to make the worm holes possible.

"Anna, you know that wasn't the reason why. Those bastards could teleport quickly out of harm's way, remember when Russia tried to shoot down the mother body when it appeared in the Bering Sea? Fucker moved out of the way just in time for the missiles to go streaking towards Alaska and California. We had to deploy counter strike measures to make sure the west coast wasn't vaporized. Almost started a third world war. Look, I know you're pissed, but the only reason we're still alive and the rest of the world is dead is because we were lucky to be in the right place at the right time. We are lucky those things, for whatever reason, do not attempt to breach the oceans. We're lucky their death lights don't work on us this far down. Parker was just unlucky. I mean come on, he had the luck of the draw that his mother was a navy helmsman stuck on shit-can duty for insubordination. He had to be born down here in this fucking shit hole, he—" But his words were cutoff as Anna struck out, a hard right-cross connecting with the middle-aged man's flabby cheeks. Randy stumbled back, bouncing off the wall.

"Whoa, whoa, whoa!" Susanna cried out, and got between them. Randy didn't retaliate, he just held his right cheek and laughed. It was clear he'd been on the sauce all day. His drinking had gotten worse over the past year. How in the hell he managed to develop alcoholism in these conditions was absurd.

"Fuck you, Randy. At least Parker didn't try and take the coward's way out. He died because he took an extra five minutes to find your fucking booze. You don't think we don't see what you're doing, staying lit on that rot gut? We both know the only reason you haven't put a bullet in your brain yet is because you're afraid of puncturing the hive walls. Don't wanna screw us over when you decide to show us you have no fucking spine. Ain't that right, Ran?" Anna fired back. Randy ceased laughing, his glazed eyes glaring at her with intense hatred.

"Look, we've been stuck down here for years in a space no bigger than my old apartment. Humans weren't designed to live in such cramped confines for so long. The fact we are still alive is a miracle, not just luck. You guys need to remember that," Susannah had said in a calm, level voice. Neither crew member responded to this. She looked to Randy. "Sober up and then make sure the sub comes back with the equipment and the suit." Anna's eyes widened at this. Susan moved on before she could reply. "Look, I know it's fucked up, but it's the only EVO suit we have, and unless we want to starve to death, we need that thing back. It's not the first time we've retrieved it from the surface… like this." Randy nodded and skulked off down the corridor leading to the sub bay. When he was gone, she went and grabbed Anna, bear hugging her. At first Anna resisted, and then she went limp, and began to sob, her crying echoing off the metal walls.

It was two weeks later that they made contact with the sub crew. Anna had been sitting in her bunk, rereading the note that had been found in the EVO suit pocket. She assumed Parker had grabbed it while rummaging through the ship.

To whoever finds this, my name is Anthony Burgess, Captain of the HMS Burke. I know now we were sent on a suicide mission to get the creature's attention drawn away from Her Majesty's port. The creatures, we know now they are attracted to electronic signals and certain wave lengths emitted by our computers. We were in the middle of the Atlantic when we found out that parliament was no more. London had fallen, as had most of Europe. I've tried pinging ports of call all over the world... No response. We've been at sea for weeks now, keeping our engines shut off for fear of attracting them. My men think me crazy, and I fear a mutiny may form at any moment, that they will storm the bridge and force me to turn on the engines. I will not. I've seen the news clips, the footage from the cities. What a horrible way to die. I can't, I won't I will no—

"Hey Anna, come down to the comms bay ASAP. You need to see this," Susanna's voice came through her walkie talkie. Anna put the note away and got up. She was still reeling from her son's death, was forced to recall the vivid memories of when she'd just found out she was pregnant. It was her first week in the research labs, tasked with observing thermal vent openings in the ocean floor for the big oil companies, who by then practically owned the US military industrial complex. It was basically busy work for inferiors such as her who had been demoted or were fresh recruits. She should have been on a nuclear sub, making a six-figure salary by keeping tabs on the Russians. Then they found out about her heritage—the paranoia was at new cold war levels—and she ended up here. She remembered watching the video transmissions from the surface, back when their small satellite TV still worked. The grainy footage showing the huge lumbering mass, stretching miles across in either direction, hovering above the skyline of Manhattan. The way the camera zoomed into the streets, where the crowds of human beings burst into so much red mist in the wake of the violet death lights. The way entire streets had been painted red, before the footage went to static.

"What is it?" Anna asked as she ducked into the comms room. Half the monitors were black, many of the external cameras breaking down over the years without maintenance, but on the remaining screens she could see the still images of a huge submarine passing by. There was large faded lettering on the side that looked to be Russian. "Holy shit. When was this?" she asked, her eyes wide at the image. It was the first time she'd seen a submersible other than their own pass by the research lab since... when? 2020? 2021? She couldn't remember, except that Parker had just been a toddler back then.

"About four hours ago. They tried to ping us but everyone was asleep. There's a problem though," she said, her voice tense and controlled, the way she sounded when informing the surface crew of a floater inbound.

"Problem?" Anna asked, and at this Randy came bleary-eyed into the station, reeking of booze and old sweat.

"The fuck's going on? Why'd you wake me up?" Randy asked.

"A Russian submarine, call sign Kop'ye Poseydona, pinged us four hours ago. They managed to hack SAM-V and are using him as collateral. They wanna talk, or, I think they said, 'Identify yourselves.' I don't know, my Russian is shit, I only know standard maritime call signs." She pointed to the ratty copy of the navy maritime sailor's handbook, shrugging.

"What the fuck!? They hacked SAM? I didn't even know he could be—" Randy exclaimed.

"Anything with a motherboard and two-way router can be hacked," Anna interrupted. Randy rubbed the bridge of his nose and squeezed his eyes shut. Anna studied the screens intensely, where three alternating photos and one grainy film showed SAM-V, their only means of getting supplies from the surface back down here, floating lazily away from the docking bay on the east side of the station, where it eventually married with the massive black sub via a retractable docking platform.

"I haven't replied to them yet. Figured I'd wait for you all and see what we should do," Susannah said.

"Tell them we need that fucking sub back. Without it we're as good as dead," Randy said, fright cutting through his hangover, slamming reality home into his soaked brain.

"Yeah, but how? I don't know Russian," Susannah said. Anna continued staring at the screens in disbelief at what she saw.

"I...I do. It's the reason why I was put down here in the first place," Anna said. "That's a Borei-class nuclear attack sub. Their call sign is Poseidon's Spear." She laughed at the bitter irony of it all.

"Jesus, I gotta be dreaming still. Were you some kind of spy, Anna?" Randy asked incredulously.

"No. But the military had their suspicions, before the floaters came. We were at the brink of war with the Russian Federation. My family immigrated from Novosibirsk when I was only a baby, my father was an ex-pat who came to work for the US Army as a nuclear scientist. My name before they Americanized it was Anastasia Chernov. A lot of espionage was going on at the time on both sides. They couldn't outright court martial me for something they had no proof of, so they stuck all of us who were even remotely Russian in jobs like this, where no vital information could—oh fuck it, I don't have time to explain it all." Anna bent down to speak into the microphone.

"What'd you just say?" Randy asked as Susannah dialed in the frequency that the identification command had come in through before hitting the send button.

"I told them we're an American, *civilian* research lab and that we pose no threat to them, and that we'd very much like our submarine back," Anna said. They all sat in tense silence waiting for a reply. Several minutes passed, and Anna was about to send another message when a harsh Russian voice crackled through the speakers. The two crew members studied Anna's poker face as she listened.

"Well?" Randy asked impatiently.

"They gave us an ultimatum. They ordered us to get aboard SAM when he returns, in which they will bring us back to the submarine. If we don't comply, they will blow us up, to put it simply," Anna said. As if a portent to her message, the school bus yellow sub came into view of the cameras, being controlled with the erratic movement of someone operating an unfamiliar piece of equipment. Eventually however, the Russian operated SAM-V managed to find its way back to the loading dock.

"Fuck, what do they want with us?!" Randy exclaimed. "They're bluffing, it's been twenty something years since human warfare fell out of style."

"No, those subs were built just before the floaters came. I remember how the navy was scared shitless of them," Anna said. "Each one has enough nuclear torpedoes and MIRV missiles to lay waste to half the country's aircraft carriers."

"Doska, seychas!" The speaker barked, causing everyone to jump.

"We gotta go, now. Susannah, do you still have that Colt?" Anna asked as they raced through the bulkhead towards the docking bay.

ANNA THOUGHT she was going to have a panic attack on her way to the sub. SAM was designed to hold one person and a stash of cargo at most, so their uncertain future, coupled with the gun butt digging into her stomach and the sardine can environment of the sub put her within a hair's breadth of a meltdown. Somehow she held on, keeping her composure. Susannah was her stalwart stoic self, and seeing her react inspired Anna. She knew the woman's service record was heavily redacted, but seeing her cool, calm demeanor in so many instances of shit-hitting-the-fan suggested special forces or black ops.

As they neared the sub, she whispered in Anna's ear while Randy repeatedly muttered a prayer.

"SAM is probably bugged, so keep your voice low. Depending on what we find in there, we could take them over. Being cramped in that tube for that long probably means they're half crazy. Watch their faces when we get in. Look for signs of vitamin deficiencies, the way they hold their guns. Did you get much experience with firearms training as a sailor?"

"No, well… other than firing m4s off the bow of a kitty hawk to pass the time," Anna said, her voice trembling. There was an abrupt halt as SAM docked with the submarine.

"Alright. Take my lead. If I blink three times fast, that means shit is about to go south. Aim for center mass. Hope your Russian is fluent," Susannah said as the bulkhead from SAM was opened.

The first thing they saw was the rusted barrel of an AK-47 being shoved in their faces.

"Vykhod!" a hoarse voice barked.

"Go," Anna said. Susannah put her hands up and allowed herself to be pulled out of the vertical porthole. Randy was next, followed by Anna, who made sure to wear the baggiest shirt she could find to hide the Colt. She prayed they would not spot the snub nose and boot dagger Susannah had squirreled away.

The first thing that hit her was the miasma of man stink and burnt engine grease that permeated the humid, warm hull. They were huddled against a wall, a rifle barrel trained on them. The man who held the gun was incredibly gaunt, eyes sunken and bloodshot, the remains of his black uniform sweat-stained and tattered. Anna could see his skin, how incredibly pale it was, and understood the sub's crew probably didn't surface much, given the nuclear reactors that would throw off an enormous energy source. It was still unclear how or why the floaters were attracted to the electrical signatures of man-made machines, but Anna knew nuclear reactors were the first places the floaters showed up. The reports of reactors failing across the country and remaining reactors ordered to be shut down immediately were the first of many signs that the creatures were attracted to energy.

Anna asked him why they forced her and her comrades to board the sub, knowing they posed no threat. His response surprised her. He had the glint of madness in his eyes as he spoke, but this softened to a miserable sadness as he gave his answer.

"It has…been so long since we've encountered other people. We've been sailing for years, ordered to maintain strict radio silence from our superiors until the order to unleash the salvo was given," he said in Russian, and Anna knew that order never came.

"Are you aware that the Russian Federation is no more? There are no orders to give… The surface is uninhabitable. There is no war," Anna said.

"What are you—" Susannah began before the man barked incredulously at her.

"Lies! Fucking American pigs! You lie! Mother Russia will never fall! Russia will—" He began to scream, the rifle trembling in his hands. Susannah moved so quick that Anna didn't realize what had happened until the man was on the ground, twitching, the hilt of her boot dagger sticking out of the side of the man's neck. He squeezed the trigger of his gun reflexively, and a sporadic burst of gunfire was fired into the floor, the bullets ricocheting off steel, the report thunderous in the small echoing hull.

"Holy-fucking-shit! Holy-fucking-SHIT!" Randy yelled, holding his hands against his ears. Even though Anna's ears rang from the gun, she could hear and feel the thud of boots approaching them. Susannah scooped up the gun, and flattened herself against the side of the bulkhead just as another burst of gunfire tore through the corridor. An exposed pipe just above Randy's head began to spit steam as it was punctured. He screamed, and scrabbled out into the corridor, his hands upraised in surrender. Anna tried to grab out and stop him, but it was too late.

"Please, don't shoot! I'm not with these crazy bitches, please don't—" he began, before his plea was cut off by a single shot. Anna put a hand to her mouth as she saw most of Randy's alcohol-soaked brains fly out the back of his skull, his head rocking back from the force of the impact. For a moment he stood, a puzzled look on his face, slowly backpedaling until he slipped in his own gray matter and blood, falling against the wall. For the first time since meeting her so long ago on her first day in the labs, Anna saw something in Susan's face crack, change. There was no need for the blink signal, they both knew they'd crossed the point of no return.

The volley of fire stopped, and again boots came forward, clanking off the metal walkway, advancing slowly, cautiously. Susan looked across from Anna, both of them flattened against each side of the bulkhead. She held up a closed fist. *Wait on my signal.* The boots came closer, stopped a few feet ahead of them. There came one more cautious step, and that's when Susan gave a sharp nod to Anna. Her heart pounding, her vision narrowing, time slowing down, she and Susannah both erupted from the sides of the narrow passage way, she squeezing the trigger of the Colt, the sound of it buried under the *rata-tat-tat* of assault rifles. She felt an angry hornet pass by her ear as the Colt kicked in her hands, then a hot knife of pain as a bullet grazed off her hip. The two blurred shapes in front of them danced and twitched, before collapsing to the ground.

She turned and saw that Susannah had been hit. She stood leaning against the wall, clutching at her left arm, blood oozing from between her fingers.

"Damn, I almost forgot how much it sucks getting shot at," Susannah said through clenched teeth. She held out the rifle. "Take it, finish this. Then maybe you can get your wish after all." Anna took the gun, and put an arm around Susan. She pulled Susan back behind the bulkhead, both of them ignoring Randy's corpse.

"Here," Anna said, taking off her baggy shirt and using it like a tourniquet as she tied it tightly around the woman's upper arm. She saw where the bullet tore through the bicep, no doubt nicking an artery on its destructive flight path. Somewhere deep in the sub, an alarm bell rang. She figured they'd hit something important with all the lead flying around in the sub's guts. She'd worry about that later.

"If you find the captain, try and take him alive. We can use him," Susannah said, and then shoved Anna away. "Now go."

SHE PROCEEDED DOWN THE WALKWAY, the gun thrust out ahead of her. She clumsily checked the magazine before proceeding and saw it was about half full, she guessed around seven rounds remained. Anna checked the guns of the soldiers they'd just killed, but each magazine was empty. She passed through the bunk quarters where several canvas hammocks were strung up in rows along the wall, as well as personal lockers. She counted eight hammocks, but so far only three men were dead. *Fuck, there's no way I can kill them all,* she thought miserably. She searched for more ammo but didn't find any. She continued down past the engine room, checking corners slowly. Nothing. She went through a narrow galley and kitchen area, the smell of old fried meat blending with the diesel fuel smell, making her nauseas. *Where the hell are they?*

She had crossed most of the submarine's interior and hadn't spotted another soldier. Finally she came to the walled-off section that read CONTROL ROOM in Russian. The bulkhead door leading to it was slightly ajar. She stood next to the wall and pried the door open with the tip of the rifle barrel, expecting a barrage of bullets. Suddenly she felt the whole submarine begin to vibrate, jolting forward with an abrupt sense of movement. Someone had just made a drastic course correction.

"You can shoot me if you want, I don't fucking care!" an old voice croaked. Anna peaked her head through the door, heart slamming as she anticipated a round through the skull. Instead she saw a lone man in what was once a white captain's uniform sitting atop a rotating seat. He had a pistol in his hand, but it was not aimed at Anna.

"Drop it," she said. He laughed, shook his head.

"You claimed you were Americans, yet here I am, conversing in my mother tongue. The first humans I've seen in years other than my remaining crew, and you speak Russian. What a world."

"Where's the rest of your crew? I counted eight beds. We only killed three men. I don't want to kill the rest, but I will if you make me," she said, and he let out another croaked laugh, a sound of hysteria.

"Oh, Ivan, Nikkita and the others? Why, we shit them out a few months ago," he said, and cackled at his own deranged wit. "You see, food stores ran low. They prepared us for a long journey, but not quite... *this*, long. God has finally come to pass judgement on us. He saw what you westerners were turning our world into, and he sent us the sky creatures. They are gods, you know. Elders. This is our rapture. I used to think...that the mission was all that mattered, but now...I see we were not meant to live. We are a scourge on this planet, and they are the clean-up crew." He raised the gun, pointing it towards his own head.

"Don't. Put it down," Anna commanded, still processing what she'd just heard. She now realized these men probably meant to take them prisoner and eat them, and she had to swallow hard to keep from vomiting up the shitty tasting MRE she'd eaten a couple hours ago.

"No. I've been running from the gates of Hell ever since I first tasted the flesh of man. I know what awaits me," he said, putting the barrel of the revolver under his chin, pulling the trigger. The roof of his skull exploded, painting several blinking lights and switches with blood, brain and bone.

"Goddamnit!" Anna shouted as she saw that their depth gauge was shrinking rapidly. The son of a bitch was making them surface. She could see the external camera's mounted on the periscope showing them ascending rapidly. She gazed over at the controls, trying to get a lay of the land. She knew this particular type of submarine had been reverse engineered from a captured US Sea-wolf class submarine back in the early 2000's. It had been years since she'd looked at the control panel of one of those subs, but her training was long and arduous, the US Navy making sure their nuclear sub pilots knew the schematics and operations in their sleep.

She closed her eyes, trying to remember what the controls looked like from her time training on the *USS Carter*. She slowed her breathing, forcing herself to calm down, and there it was, in her mind. When she opened her eyes, she saw that the control room was indeed nearly identical to the Sea-wolf's control room. Except there was one problem. The captain's brains and blood had seeped into the depth gauge control panel, short-circuiting depth controls, and the screen showing their approximate location below the surface had gone glitchy.

She was thrown about then as the submarine violently surfaced, bouncing around in the chop of the Pacific Ocean. She looked and could see the waves washing over the bow of the sub. They were officially exposed. She could see from the roof and periscope cameras that the skies were clear, for now. But they were stuck up here. Unless…

SHE'D SPRINTED through the narrow walkways and nearly slipped on the large pool of blood as she came into the docking bay room, where Susannah lay sprawled, her body the death gray of cigarette ash, at least three pints of blood escaping her and painting the floor of the sub. She looked up dazedly at Anna. *Jesus, how long did I leave her here for?*

"Did you...Get em' all?" she asked with a weak voice. At first Anna didn't reply, she was staring down at the water filled sealed bulkhead where the entrance to SAM once was.

"What...what happened? Why is this sealed off?" she asked. Susannah shrugged, and then winced at the pain it caused her.

"Guess we were moving at a pretty good clip...SAM got torn off as whoever was piloting this fucker started hauling ass. Water began to gush in before an emergency breach protocol...or something caused the bulkhead to seal itself. Poor Sammy, down there all alone, floating aimlessly," she said, and then let out a deep sigh, and closed her eyes.

"No," Anna said, and wanted to scream. But she didn't have the energy for that. She felt used up, completely exhausted, and felt she could lie down right next to Susannah and fade away to oblivion. But another alarm snapped her out of that. She went to Susannah.

"Come on, there's gotta be a medkit down here somewhere. I can..." But the mysterious woman she'd been bunking with for years put a finger to her lips, shaking her head weakly.

"Please, let me die. I'd rather bleed out than..." she began, but her head lolled back. Anna knew what she was going to say, and started to cry. Except this time Susannah didn't have the strength to hold her.

"Susannah," she said, but the woman was unresponsive. The alarm kept blaring. Gently, she laid Susan back down, smoothing her hair and kissing her forehead before retracing the journey she just took.

In the control room, she saw on the video screens that the sky was no longer clear blue. A massive shadow had blotted out the sun, and the camera's night vision turned everything a grainy green. She could see the bloated, slow-moving form perhaps a mile or so above in the sky. She saw the tentacles slowly descending from the huge abdomen, knowing at any minute the dead lights would turn on and she'd succumb to the horrible death that claimed most of the human population.

Ignoring the cameras, she prowled the weapons control panel, thankfully the payload inventory screen was still working. She could see the sub was equipped with ten MIRV nuclear warheads. The screen didn't list how many megatons each warhead was, but she assumed it would be enough to take at least one of the big bastards out. She went about arming all ten missiles, having to grab the two keys off the dead captain and insert them into special red compartments, what her sailor friends in the navy jokingly called "FUBAR boxes," which allowed submarine captains to initiate manual override in case they had to operate autonomously. Once this was done, the screen flashed with a warning sign indicating that the nuclear payloads were prepped for launch, and requested assignable targets.

She panicked at first when she saw she could only assign geographic coordinates, but then saw the ACTIVE TARGETS option, which she assumed was meant for moving targets such as aircraft carriers or US bombers.

"Thank fucking god," she said as she highlighted this. A new screen came up, a list of potential targets highlighted on a radar. She saw two huge blips on the screen, the one just above her and another creature some fifteen miles away, coming closer. She grinned. She knew the missiles carried multiple warheads each and could split off to hit different targets once the booster was discarded in midflight. Anna selected five missiles to each target just as she began to feel light-headed, her vision blurring as her eyeballs started to feel too big for their sockets. *Warning: Targets are located within the blast radius of this module. Continue?* the screen read. She grinned, and hit the two red buttons labelled LAUNCH on each side of the control panel. A moment later a new siren started, red lights flashing in the control room. She watched through the periscope as a large compartment opened where the hull once was, and a moment later her vision was obscured by smoke as the rockets fired away.

Using the last of her fading strength, she climbed up the ladder and through the porthole of the submarine's conning tower, and as she exited, she was engulfed in smoke. Instantly she felt the death light's effects, her blood beginning to boil and her skin quivering as her carbon elements began to break down. She collapsed on the domed hull behind her, and saw as the ten pillars of smoke turned to twenty, a cluster of them racing far to the left, where another body loomed over the horizon. But she was focused on the one right in front of her.

She saw as the warheads plunged into the body, which seemed to be gelatinous in the way the missiles simply sunk into it. For a horrifying moment she thought the beast would disable the missiles using its bizarre interdimensional anatomy. But a split second later there came a wonderful orange blossom from the middle of the massive floating body, followed by several smaller fireballs. She grinned as the white flash enveloped her.

Mama's coming, baby. I'll be there soon.

3

CONFLAGRATION

To this day, the therapist that Gus and I were advised to see calls it a stress-induced group hallucination. A small part of myself wants to believe her. It was sure as shit stressful, being surrounded by literal walls of flame, the inside of your suit reaching a hundred something degrees, the roar of all-consuming fire screaming in your ears when your squad mates weren't yelling commands at you over their shoulders. Conditions to which we had been subjected to for hours on end. *We* being one of the many squadrons called on that day to beat back one of the worst wildfires in fifty years. For a while I was willing to entertain the notion that me and my colleagues, some of the best firemen in the state of California and all mentally sound, could have temporarily lost our minds and all seen the same things that weren't actually there. Yet when I close my eyes at night, trying to find momentary reprieve in sleep, I see it. The thing which makes my pink, burned skin crawl with horror.

It's hard to talk about the things I've seen with anyone, which I guess is part of the reason I'm writing it down. Everyone has this flowery romantic depiction of fire fighters. We're the brave, brass-balled heroes who fight the fires, save the day and get all the glory. When you try and tell someone you have PTSD from being a fire fighter, you tend to get that look. These people don't think about the fact that a disturbing amount of the fires I've been called to fight weren't always put out in time. I've been an unwilling witness to so many exhibitions of human destruction.

I had been a firefighter for ten years prior to the Angel's Pass incident that nearly broke my mind. I saw my first dead body a year into the job. Apartment fire. We got there just in time to stop the whole complex from being burned, but three units were a total loss. Once the blaze was extinguished, we went about clearing out the three units, and in the first one we had discovered the cause of the fire and who had started it.

Ignition point was the oven in a small one-bedroom studio apartment, reduced to ash, walls blackened, the stove open. Sitting sprawled to a charred Lazy Boy, the flesh melted into the exposed metal springs of the chair, was a body almost completely charred over. The face still had some cooked skin on it, a few patches of glazed brown hide around the whitish gleam of skull. Sticking out of the charred arm, which hung down to the side, was a blackened metal syringe tip, the adjoining plastic tube and plunger a hardened melted mass on the floor. Overdose, either heroin or some other manufactured poison. Then we had gone into the bedroom, where someone had found the charred metal skeleton of a baby pen, and the small, blackened mass that lay curled up in its center.

Once, our station was called to help assist on a high-rise blaze, a twenty story hotel called Isle Mystique located in Oakland. It was freshly built by a contractor who had skimped on the design because, as we would later learn, he had called in a few favors from a good friend who happened to be a city inspector. As a result, the half-assed installed extinguisher system failed critically when one of the units caught fire on the tenth floor. Turned out to be a bad circuit that threw some sparks next to exposed insulation. What should have been an easily extinguished quirk of architecture turned into a full-on blaze when our trucks rolled up to throw water, and I had noticed a few crimson streaks on the ground where people had jumped from windows trying to escape. As we hooked up to the nearest hydrant and waited for the hose to get pressurized, I saw someone ablaze hurl themselves out over the deck of the room they were trapped in, a human comet streaking to the ground.

The fall wasn't bad enough to kill her, but you couldn't tell by looking at the body. Someone immediately doused her in water, but by then it was too late. The fatty epidermal layer of her skin had been burned away in most places, leaving splotchy pink patches that faded into twitching exposed muscle tissue. Her eyeballs had exploded, the two sockets a gluey mess of hollowed-out gore, the skull smashed and leaking cooked brains onto the hot California asphalt. Her legs were a broken ruin beneath her, the gleam of white bone poking through shiny skin like an overcooked bratwurst stabbed by a skewer.

I only reflect on these horrors because it's important to show that I was no stranger to death and trauma by the time the wildfires began cooking the state alive. Even during those previous horrible scenes of human suffering, I did not witness anything paranormal or extraordinary while on duty, or suffer breaks from reality.

IT WAS in August when we got called out. Small scrub fires had been popping up all over the state that year because of the record-breaking drought, but luckily the winds had never been strong and the fires either died out or were quickly contained with strategically placed fire barriers. Then Angel's Pass, a section of heavily wooded hills in the southeast part of the Sonora mountains, caught fire. They could never figure out the original ignition point, as Angel's Pass is in one of the most remote parts of the state, and in that brutally hot summer very few people were hiking.

Along with that is the fact that Angel's Pass sat atop a state-protected Mojave burial ground, and people caught trespassing on the historical site were usually fined heavily. But something or someone must have started it, because within four hours, the blaze was fanning out in all directions, moving five feet a minute. Five upscale subdivisions flanked the nearest borders of the forest. Those neat and close together colonial-styled neighborhoods for the upper-class white-collar families went up like tinderboxes, much to the pleasure of the hipsters and yuppies who complained about bay area gentrification.

It soon became clear that this was going to be a big one, and with the total loss of those luxury neighborhoods, including ten people already claimed, the governor declared a state of emergency. Calls were made across the state for some of the best, strongest firefighting teams from each active station to join up and help fight the blaze. It was inevitable I would get picked, being six-four and two hundred and fifty pounds of Samoan muscle. My nickname was Big Lu because I towered above the rest of the guys in my squad. Me and two other people, Gus Ellison and Jerry Fitzpatrick, were chosen because of our experience, physical endurance and strength. Although all the guys wanted to volunteer, we needed at least half the station in working capacity in case they were needed in our jurisdiction, which happened to be thirty miles from where the blaze was eating through million-dollar homes, protected forests and everything in between.

The one-hour drive took three because we had to meander our way through the wave of evacuees fleeing the blaze. We were still some ten miles away from the rally point for our first skirmish with the blaze, but it looked like literal hell on earth from the highway. The normally bright summer sun was obscured by an obsidian haze of smoke; the orange cinders and embers rose into the sky like burning stars threatening to bring the sky down with it. I could see the ethereal bodies of airplanes flying through the smoke, being called in to do water drops on a few areas, doing little good. The heat was incredible with a blaze that size, and the water simply boiled into steam before having a chance to douse the flames.

We had to pilot our large engine around stopped cars and people wearing respirators and shirts around their heads. I had slipped my own mask on before getting out of the engine, the air smelling of burnt everything. Eventually we saw the sign and clearing for EMTs and fire fighters. We took a dirt fire road that snaked up through the valley. We passed several water tank trucks; due to the remote location, no hydrants or stationary water sources were around. We were waved to the left by men wearing respirators, and followed another dirt path. We barely had room to pull over to let the ambulance pass that came from the direction we were headed, its siren lights obscured by smoke. Eventually we came to a spot where a lone tank truck sat, and we assumed that was our cue to get out. I walked over to the lip of the ridge and saw the steady wall of flame marching towards us. I remember how hypnotic it was, staring at that massive dancing orange and yellow body through shimmering heat waves. The way the trees quite literally burst into flames before the fire even reached them, the intense heat spontaneously combusting the bone-dry pine and scrub bush like they were soaked in kerosene.

"Lumou, quit sightseeing and move your ass!" Gus called. But even then I paused, thinking I saw something. A tall, slim figure, almost as tall as the pine trees, that seemed to be made of flame, walking along the fire's edge. Like a child's primitive stick figure blown up to a massive scale and comprised entirely of fire. It seemed to glide along the edge, arms outstretched, almost...frolicking, the way you see a beautiful woman frolicking through a field of flowers in those cheesy commercials. Graceful, at ease.

"Lu! You gone fuckin deaf? We gotta soak this whole slope before that shit gets a chance to cross the road. Come on!" Jerry yelled. I did a double take towards our parked truck. Gus and Jerry were both uncoiling the connector hose, the two volunteer truck drivers, whose names I never caught, helping Jerry drag it over to the valve on the water tank. I took another quick glance back at the firewall, but lost site of the figure in the blaze, which seemed to have encroached another ten feet in the short time it took me to look at my colleagues. I ran over and got the generator going on the truck to build the water pressure. Once the hose was connected and pressure was established, we started soaking the bank directly below us, taking care not to slip down the sandy embankment towards the few remaining unburned acres.

I scanned the burning horizon fervently as I directed the hose out in a wide fan, walking to the left as I went, trying to create a wet barrier as long as I could before the hose ran out or the fire snuck up on us. I thought I could see movement to the far right, where the tree line disappeared around the curve of a small mountain. Then I heard a thunderous roar, I instinctively ducked as one of the modified DC-10s roared overhead, a bright red cascade of fire retardant blooming from its belly as it did a close pass of the eastern firewall, close to where I thought I'd seen the fire specter.

Twenty minutes into our efforts, a man wearing goggles, a respirator, and a water-soaked hoodie came flying down the dirt road on ATV, nearly colliding with Gus and Jerry, who were in the middle of the road guiding the hose along as I walked, making sure it didn't get kinked. He slid to a stop five feet from Jerry.

"We got an emergency!" the man began. I flipped the pressure release on the hose, shutting it off for a second.

"You take a look around? Half the damn state is an emergency," Jerry shouted through his respirator.

"We got a park ranger stranded two miles from here at a ranger's station. Got a broken leg and he's losing his shit over the CB. Fire is almost on him. Who's the strongest sonofabitch of you three?"

They all pointed to me, and I shrugged, looking at Gus. He nodded.

"Go on, Big Lu. Go be a hero. Enough people have died already. We got it from here," he said, taking the sputtering hose from my hands.

"Come on! We gotta haul ass if we're gonna beat this thing," the driver said. I quickly grabbed the first aid kit and a fire blanket from the truck, then climbed on back of the ATV, the suspension groaning with my added bulk.

IN WHAT SEEMED like a blur of heat, motion and burning trees, we arrived at a narrow trail. In the distance off to our left, perhaps some two hundred feet into the forest, we saw the ranger's station, which was actually a fire watchtower. Some fifty feet beyond that was the wall of the blaze; this side of the mountain was already nearly consumed. Without a word I jumped off the four-wheeler before he even came to a complete stop, and ran headlong into the blazing void. I could see the ranger halfway down the tower, sprawled out in a heap on the steps. Must have fallen trying to flee.

As I drew closer to the tower, I heard a peculiar sound over the roar of the fire. A rhythmic thumping, like an army marching in step or the mighty thump of a tribal band's bass drums. Powerful enough to make the ground shake. I hesitated in my sprint, looking to my left. My gaze fixated upon the site. What I saw still haunts my dreams.

Propelled by long spindly legs that ascended into a round fireball of an abdomen, from which jutted five or six limbs that I guess could be called arms, the entity bore down on the tower like a wide receiver sprinting towards the goal line. It was nearly as tall as the ranger station, and as it drew close I could see that it had a head. There were two coal black eyes perched atop the stubby head, which seemed devoid of a neck. If it had a mouth, I did not see it. It didn't appear to have any substance to it, no charred skin or bone structure visible through its burning limbs. I don't know whether to call it a demon, a god, or a monster. All I know was that it moved with singular purpose.

I had halted completely when I saw it run into the tower. In a sudden eruption the body dematerialized into a fireball as it seemed to go through the tower, and instantly the structure was ablaze. I ran forward, but the heat stopped me some forty feet away. I watched as the ranger rolled down the stairs wildly. I could faintly hear his screams over the dull roar of the fire. I watched with helpless horror as he crawled through the gap of safety rail between the stairs and fell two stories to the ground. He moaned and writhed on the forest floor, and managed to extinguish part of his body in the fall. I put the fire blanket around me, trying to get as close as I could to perhaps drag the man to safety. But at forty feet, the pain was unbearable; I could feel my skin broiling and my head growing foggy and delirious as heat stroke threatened to debilitate me. Then I smelled burning hair as my humble mustache and nose hairs started to singe. I took one squinting glance at the ranger, who had managed to crawl forward a small amount before dying.

His face was a blistering, charred mass of vague flesh, his skin melting from the indirect heat, much like an oven broiling steaks. He reached out one hand, bright pink and oozing blood at his fingertips, bits of burnt leaves and dirt embedded in the raw, cooked flesh as he tried to drag himself across the ground. His polyester and rayon ranger's uniform had melted to his body, bubbling up instead of burning away like cotton. He opened his blackened mouth to scream, and that's when I saw his head twitch, little explosions sending bits of white shards out of his mouth as his molars exploded, a phenomenon I had heard about but never actually witnessed. His eyes, which were already bulging out of his head in a ridiculous parody of shocked surprise, burst, the insides running and steaming down his face like half-cooked egg whites.

I had to peel myself away from the horror as the fire started to surround me. I could hear the driver of the ATV shouting for me and I turned to run. The flames were on either side and threatening to surround me if I didn't get to the roadway in time. I ran, my lungs burning as they inhaled hot, smoky air. I somehow managed to make it to the road, nearly collapsing before I got to the four-wheeler. The driver grabbed me and steadied my large mass as I sat down heavily on the rear edge of the seat.

"Take me back to my squadron," I said, and held on to him as he floored it, trying to escape the heat and outrun the blaze. That's when I lost consciousness.

I WAS AWAKENED BY GUS, who was looming over me. There was an oxygen mask on my face. I was lying on the ground, confused as to where I was. It felt like I was inside a furnace.

"Jesus, man, I thought we almost lost you." His face was pouring sweat; all color had drained from it. "Come on, get up, we need you. No time for a hospital. We gotta get the hell out of here!" he yelled as Jerry appeared. Both of them pulled me to my feet with a grunt of effort. The ATV driver was gone. We were somewhere along the dirt road. The fire blazed on either side of us. I stood unsteadily and saw that the tank truck was ahead of us, still married to our fire truck via the connector hose.

"Where are the others?" I asked.

"The drivers had to be evaced out, got heat stroke. We need help disconnecting the hose so we can scram," Gus said.

I noticed that a couple gallons of water had leaked from the hose connector, and the dirt road had transformed into a small mud pit where the fire engine was. As me and Jerry walked over to the tank truck, I heard it, that familiar thudding. I froze up, and turned around. Through the tops of the trees I could make out fast movement.

"Man, we've been hearing that damn thumping all day. What *is* that?" Jerry asked, looking around.

"We need to go, right now." I ran over and quickly began twisting off the connector valve. A spray of hot water shot out as the remaining fluid from the hose flowed out the empty end, soaking my pants. I ran back over to the truck, quickly reeling in the connector hose while Jerry and Gus reeled in the main hose. The thumping grew closer, and I could see the form coming through the burning trees.

I screamed at them, "Get the truck going! Fucking demon or something!" It was all I could think to say, and either the expression on my face or the lack of color in my normally dark skin must've scared Gus, because he stopped reeling in the hose, looking over his shoulder to see the impossible form running through the trees. With ten feet of hose still hanging off, a sacrilegious act among trained fire fighters, he ran into the driver's cab. The throaty roar of the diesel engine coming to life spoke over the sound of that terrible thumping cacophony. Jerry stood mesmerized at the thirty-foot form growing up from the wall of flames like the devil himself, knocking over burning trees like they were saplings and approaching us.

"Jerry, come on!" I screamed, running up the side of the truck's cab. Unlike other fire trucks, ours carried a chemical retardant which was disbursed via a hydraulic nozzle station perched atop the truck like a gunner's turret. This was due to our station's proximity to the commuter airstrips located a few miles southeast of Santa Cruz. I prayed the reservoir of chemical foam was full. Luckily, it was. The truck started moving, the whole frame shuddering as Gus tried to maneuver the engine through the mud pit and heavily rutted road. I watched as Jerry stood like a deer in the headlights, his vacuous gaze following the fire behemoth. It reached the road, bursting out through the tree line just as the truck crawled its way out of the mud, all six wheels finding traction. The engine roared like a metallic beast as Gus floored it, and I watched helplessly as the thing bore down on Jerry. He didn't move as the being, a horrifying monstrosity that resembled a hastily drawn spider on two legs, shot out one thin burning pilon of an arm. Blazing, ethereal appendages like fingers disappeared into Jerry's midsection.

It was an almost instantaneous thing. I would hazard maybe a second after the thing speared Jerry, he exploded. It was as if he'd ingested a couple sticks of dynamite and lit the fuse on the way down. I ducked as a burning piece of his arm came flying at me, the cauterized stump hitting me in the face, leaving the circular scar I still have today on my left cheek. Burning chunks of Jerry came raining down, and the smell of boiling blood and burnt polyester uniform cut through the smoke.

Then it was charging at the truck, long skinny legs propelling it forward with ease. Understanding I was about to die a horrible death, I depressed the pressure release button and aimed the tapered mouth of the nozzle at its midsection. For a moment nothing happened. Then a small sputter of white foam shot out. I almost wanted to laugh because of how ridiculous this all was. I was about to fight a giant paranormal fire creature using chemical retardant meant for putting out jet fuel fires, and the damn thing didn't even work. For a split second I thought I might be going crazy, until I felt the heat radiating off the being like it was the surface of the sun. I cringed back, but kept my hand on the nozzle. Right as the thing reached out one long arm towards the truck, a beautiful white jet of PhostrEx agent arced out of the nozzle, right into the midriff of the hellish being.

Things happened very rapidly then. I remember the way the foam quickly expanded, the way it's supposed to in order to snuff out the fuel source. The thing collapsed in on itself, the limbs losing substance and falling like a collapsing camp fire. I aimed the nozzle up to increase the arc as the truck sped away, rounding a corner in the fire trail. Then I saw as the thoroughly covered mass blossomed in one giant foamy mushroom cloud before the second explosion happened. I don't remember much except a white flash, which was bright enough to burn a small hole in my left cornea. I was knocked unconscious from the blast, and according the Gus it felt like the shockwave from an atom bomb had hit the truck. He had to fight to keep it from flying off the road.

When I woke up again, I was in the hospital, being treated for a concussion and second-degree burns on my arms and face, with a small black hole in my vision.

IT WAS one of the deadliest wildfires of the century. Thousands of acres ablaze, hundreds of homes destroyed. The whole ordeal took a month for the final cinders to be extinguished. Eighty people perished, twenty of them firefighters. According to the doctors, I was repeatedly ranting and raving about demons getting Jerry while I was under sedation. Gus didn't see as much as I did, but he corroborated my story about the fire entity, and on the department's orders, we both had to attend at least eight cognitive behavioral therapy sessions. Because, you know, two guys who claimed to have seen a thirty foot tall fire monster probably got a few fuckin screws loose.

What I haven't told my therapist is that in my downtime, while I sat at home, body half bandaged and looking like a Hawaiian Freddy Kruger, I began reading articles on the internet about the fires. One thing led to another and I eventually ended up on the personal blog of a reporter who was there when the blaze first erupted. She had managed to snap a few blurry photos of something moving through the wild fires. "DEMONS OF THE MOJAVE?" was the headline of the article.

I have since done my research, hours of reading through anthropological and historical texts about the Mojave people in the area, discovering the elemental gods that they, along with many other tribes across the nation, worshipped and feared. Johanna was the god of wrath, a fierce, unforgiving deity who took the form of the sun, and punished those cowardly warriors who refused to fight, as well as those that practiced the black magic of their region. If what I saw was in fact an ancient Native American god, what did that make me? A god killer? I don't know. All I know is that I'm done fighting fires. I've seen enough burned bodies and felt enough heat to know what Hell is like if I ever go there.

4

THE GOLDEN SHEPHERD

She didn't run so much as float. Her limbs were vague mechanisms, hurtling through the third dimension while her vision shifted in and out of the fourth. The walls of the corridor pulsed, breathing in sync with her own respiration. Behind her was Sister Elizabeth, the only other one of the sisters who Marie could convince to run away with her. Their foot falls echoed strangely as they ran, thudding pulses that bounced off the walls like erratic heartbeats.

Ten tabs. Ten tabs of Golden Shepherd was the initiation dose for entering The Flock. It also happened to be the dose administered when Simon felt one of his sisters needed to be shown the light, a common cure for those who proved less receptive to his aura. Although Marie's tolerance to the potent hallucinogen had undoubtedly increased since she first entered The Flock's gates, wide-eyed and drunk on the word of Simon Gabriel, the Golden Shepherd, a one of a kind serotonergic analogue, was an unstoppable train at certain doses. Everyone at the compound was on a strict micro-dosing schedule that saw the brothers and sisters averaging about three tabs over the course of a day. This was Simon's way of making sure his scripture was absorbed, *inherited*.

The hallway seemed to never end. Although trying to process time in this state was nearly impossible, some small part of her understood she had to move fast to get out the back door of the Gabriel compound before Brother Donald and Brother Dannie could come back from their group tantric love sessions, which was just a flowery name for the scheduled orgies that took place twice a week. Another part of Simon's strict regiment were these mandatory orgies for *group cohesion*, regardless of whether the sisters felt like participating.

"Up ahead," Sister Elizabeth said. Marie blinked, seeing the silhouette of a figure walking down the hallway. To Marie, the man first appeared like a flat paper cutout, before suddenly appearing ten feet in front of her. Brother David was materializing out of the ether, his big wavering hands trying to hold her down. Marie tried to focus, drawing fourth the flare of rage, the spark she had first learned to cultivate after her fourth day in the *adjustment chamber*. She could feel it charging in her brain like a bolt of lightning milliseconds before striking the ground.

"Hey…What the fuck. WHAT THE FU—" Brother David began. Marie wasn't sure how much of what she saw was hallucination and what was real, actually happening in her dimension. One second the flesh of his face was rippling, simmering and dancing around his skull like choppy waves. An unknowable amount of time later, his eyes were pulpy craters, crimson leaking from his nose. The sharp tang of urine cut through the nearly kaleidoscopic atmosphere as he collapsed on top of her.

"Fucking Christ. Come on!" Sister Elizabeth shouted, shoving the convulsing man off and grabbing at Marie with arms that felt a mile long. Marie saw the double doors materialize, growing bigger, their tan frames hanging in the wall at a strange angle. They both ran, stumbling along like newborn fawn, the ground beneath their feet feeling like the surface of a trampoline.

The first rays of sun she'd seen in days stabbed her eyes, occluding the delirious visuals with searing white light. She'd forgotten about the sun, what with being stuck in a 12x12 pitch black concrete room for four days while being fed a steady diet of Golden Shepherd and water, her fasting a necessary part of her *adjustment*.

"It's alright, just shield your eyes until we get to the forest, we have to go, Marie," Sister Elizabeth's voice came to her, hollow and distorted as if spoken from a megaphone a half mile away. Easy for her to say; she wasn't operating with her third eye pinned open and receptive to all the violent stimuli of the world. Marie felt hands pulling at her body, distant sensations that seemed to be felt through several layers of fabric, even though she was completely naked.

Eventually she was able to open her eyes to slits, the dilated pupils taking in painful glimpses of the pine forest that surrounded the compound. Sister Elizabeth ushered her towards the forest canopy, where it was dimmer among the ceiling of branches. Once there, Marie opened her eyes fully, stopping in wonder as she took in the phantasmagorical world of greens and browns and other shades of color she'd never seen before.

"Come on!" Elizabeth hissed, shoving Marie forward. She looked back at Sister Elizabeth, her visage stretched to grotesque proportions, distorting a face that Marie knew to be beautiful. They were all beautiful. Simon did not accept anything less than the most aesthetic of women to be part of his family. At least, that's how they started out.

They began to run, Marie trying not to be overwhelmed by the intense visual stimuli, by the fact she could feel the presence of every tree and shrub that surrounded her. She knew this was part of her change too. The acid, with its strange ingredients unique only to Simon's recipe, had altered something in her somehow, mutated synapses and built new receptors to allow for the constant overflow of serotonin and dopamine, which in turn had fostered her new found psionic abilities. Just like she could feel the vibrations of Sister Elizabeth's soul, the forest thrummed like high voltage livewires. Simon always said Marie was special, that she could ascend farther than any of them if she just listened to the Shepherd's word.

"Hey! Stop!" came a male voice from some distance.

"There they are!" came another. Marie looked around dazed before seeing two more silhouettes through the colorful ocean of green around them. Their black uniforms, the cloth of the brother, stood out in vivid contrast compared to the healthy green hues that surrounded them. Their presence was a violation, sacrilegious in this place of thriving natural beauty. They ran towards Marie, small devices in their hands that arced with blue fire. She could feel the electricity despite being way out of the taser's reach.

"Shit! Come on Marie!" Sister Elizabeth pleaded. But Marie stood her ground, closing her eyes. Even through her lids she could see them, feel their repulsive auras radiating like abscessed teeth in diseased gums. She focused in on the one on the right, cleansing her body of the black rage that began to fester within her after her third day in the adjustment chamber. Rage that culminated from Simon Gabriel's repeated lies, lies that only a few from the group seemed to see through.

She thought of his long luscious black hair, those handsome blue eyes, the gentle southern lilt in his voice. *You are not one being, but a piece of a collective whole that is the flock. You are only whole when in the presence of the family. You are nothing without your brothers and sisters. You. Are. Nothing.*

There came a shout as she felt the rage leave her body in a sudden violent wave, a flash like a polaroid camera, searing an after image across her corneas as the man's soul was snuffed out, his corporeal vessel obliterated by her rage. There came the sound of liquid splashing against ground, a startled scream as Brother Dillon was bathed in the hot wash of Brother Daniel's viscera.

"Holy shit," Sister Elizabeth breathed in awe. "He was right...You ascended," she said.

"The Shepherd speaks knowledge, but only those willing to listen will bear it's fruit," Marie droned, her voiced sounding insect-like to her own ears, uttering a phrase that had been played on a loop for forty-eight hours while in the adjustment chamber. She found they were the only words she could speak. She could sense the other man fleeing, his soul vibrating at the high frequency of animal terror. She couldn't let him get away though, to inform Simon of their escape.

She clenched her fist, gritted her teeth, and for a moment she left her body, travelling through the air as a black ethereal ball of energy, slamming into Brother Dillan, where his atoms destabilized rapidly, causing him to spontaneously combust. It was strange, her projected force seemed to have a different catastrophic effect on each soul.

They pressed on, Elizabeth guiding Marie through the mile or so of dense forest, trying to put as much distance between them and the compound as possible.

IT WAS NEARING dusk when they came upon the rough-cut logging road. Sister Elizabeth had an arm around Marie as they walked, the mountain air beginning to take on a chilly bite that nipped at Sister Elizabeth's skin with icy fingers. Marie didn't realize she was shivering, or that she was even cold, her brain seeming to detach itself from her parasympathetic nervous system. Despite the dimming light she could see just fine, her body still connected to the forest via unseen veins and tendons that bloomed within her every time her bare feet touched the earth.

They walked along the brown vein of road, not knowing where they were headed. All the sisters were blindfolded on their rare trips to and from the compound for provisions, which as far as Sister Elizabeth could tell was in one of the most remote parts of Idaho she'd ever seen. A vivid night sky could be seen through the broken canopy of coniferous forest as they walked. Once, they had to jump off the road, waiting behind two thick evergreen trees while a truck passed at a slow crawl, its diesel engine grumbling like a feral beast, a terrible sound that almost made Marie scream.

They let it pass and continued walking, until the dirt road eventually terminated at the shoulder of a two lane paved road. Marie saw a sign that glimmered with holographic brilliance, a symbol on it. She stared in wonder.

"Oh thank fucking Christ. We're almost there, Marie," she heard Sister Elizabeth say, rapturous joy in her voice. She focused on the symbol. Where had she seen it before? After a moment, it came to her. H. It was an H, but she couldn't comprehend what an H was. There was another sign just underneath it, filled with symbols, and she was vaguely horrified at the fact that she couldn't read. What normal people saw as "Twin Falls-6 miles" she saw as a confusing amalgamation of curves and lines.

"Here comes a car! Hide, Marie, let me try and flag them down."

VIRGIL WHITAKER YAWNED as he piloted his Chevy down the winding Highway H, fresh off a shift from the lumber mill and ready to go home, crack a few beers and get some shut eye, so he could do it all again tomorrow. He was thinking about which fast food joint he was going to stop at once he got into town when his high beams illuminated the woman on the side of the road. He almost had to swerve to keep from hitting her as she flailed her arms about.

He braked to a stop some twenty feet past where she was and reversed, getting ready to chew her out for running out in front of a truck going fifty miles-an-hour, but his aggravated response froze on his lips when he saw the skinny husk of a woman running up to his passenger window.

"Uh…Ma'am? What the hell—"

"Please, PLEASE! You have to help us. Me and my friend, we're running away from him. He's looking for us. Please, we're not crazy. Just let us ride with you for a few miles, I'm begging you," the woman pleaded. She was young, perhaps late twenties, red hair hanging in a messy corona around her head. She wore a soiled nightgown that was once white, with a peculiar symbol on it that Virgil could of swore he'd seen somewhere before.

"Whoa there, okay, okay. Just take it easy," he said, unlocking the door. She immediately opened it before disappearing behind some bushes. Virgil got out and stopped in his tracks when he saw the naked woman that materialized from the forest. "My god," he said, when he saw the multitude of scars that were etched into the alabaster flesh. It was the same symbol the woman had on her nightgown, branded into the woman's body hundreds of times. "Jesus. Okay…Just get in. I'm taking you all to the cops," he said. For a moment he locked eyes with the naked woman and froze, feeling something peculiar wash over him. Her eyes were wide, almost glowing, like the eyes of a cat in a spotlight. He found that looking directly into them made him feel light-headed, almost delirious.

"I, uh, come on," he said, forcing himself to break eye contact and walking back to his truck.

Marie sat in the back of the truck, the man giving her his coat, which smelled of wood shavings and old sweat. She tried not to vomit as the motion of the truck pulled her through time and space at a frightening speed. She knew she had to stop Simon. *The cops*, that phrase sounded familiar, she couldn't remember what they were, but she knew they were instrumental to stopping him. But what of herself? She was no longer human, she understood that much. When she looked at Sister Elizabeth, she noticed the woman would not meet her gaze. Like she was afraid of Marie. She sensed fear in the woman's soul now too. Fear and confusion.

What have I become? She wonders as the truck hurled down the road, the driver unknowingly carrying the catalyst for the next step in human evolution.

5

OBSIDIAN

It was four in the morning when Agnes Mayberry was awoken from a thin sleep by what she first thought was a thunderclap. A great crashing had sounded throughout the old house, and she could faintly hear the excited patter of paws on wood as her three cats ran around the house in an agitated frenzy. Getting up on swollen, painful feet that had been gnarled and disfigured by years of reoccurring gouty arthritis, she moaned, shuffling to put on her night robe, nearly tripping over Buttercup, who had been crouched by the wall next to her bed. The cat hissed and ran to the opposite side of the room, her hackles up.

"Oh, you poor thing. It's just some thunder, Buttercup," she said in that frail, shaky voice, the weak old woman voice she hated but had no power to change. Her jaw clenched as she made the painful journey to her wheelchair, trying to minimize the time spent on her crystal-packed joints that were more red and swollen most days than not. She sighed as her large frame landed in the seat, and she wheeled herself over to the window. The sky was clear, a blinking array of stars shining clearly in the night. No thunder or even rain.

"Well that's odd. What happened, Buttercup? Did one of you silly kitties knock one of mama's trinkets over? Ohhh, I bet you did," she said to the brown and white spotted cat, whose fur was still raised, her ears sunk flat against her skull. Of all three cats, Buttercup was the least temperamental and mean spirited. To see her wound-up like this made a pang of anxiety race through her heart. *Intruder* came to her mind, but she quickly dismissed it. Living this far out in the country in a small house made burglary uncommon. Still, she grabbed the little .22 pistol she kept in the nightstand next to her bed, and wheeled herself out to the hallway, where she hobbled over to the wall-mounted chair that took her downstairs at a snail's pace.

As she settled herself in and the whir of the electric motor marked her glacial descent, she noticed the baseball sized hole in the wall cattycorner to the one the chair was attached to. Through it she could see the faint glow of the lone street light that marked the beginning of her driveway meeting with County Road 357.

"What the blazes?" she said as she descended. When she got to the bottom, she flipped on both light switches and the canned foyer lights came on. She gasped as she saw the crater in the living room floor some ten feet away from the wall that had the hole in it. She hobbled over to it, and bent down to examine the black patch where the tan cat urine-stained carpet once was. A shiny, black object was embedded into the floorboards, having destroyed the surrounding carpet upon impact.

She straightened up and looked at the hole in the wall, then at the impact site in the floor. Gears turned slowly in her head and she realized whatever this black thing was, it had been travelling with enough force to blast through the brick and drywall and embed itself into the floorboard. She realized then with some bewilderment that this was probably a chunk of space rock. At this, she hobbled over to the kitchen, where she passed Misty and Patty, who were huddled underneath one of the kitchen chairs, their ears flattened and low growls sounding in their throats, the slit pupils staring across the room at the black aberration in the floor.

Bracing herself against the counter, Agnes rummaged through the various drawers until she came upon the small claw hammer, an artifact from her old life with Bernard, who had fancied himself a handyman. Finding what she was looking for, she retraced her agonized steps back into the foyer, wishing she had remembered to bring her wheelchair down with her. The old woman grunted as she sat herself down on the carpeted floor, and tried to wedge the claw end of the hammer into the edge of the impact site.

Buttercup watched from one of the upper risers as Agnes tried for several minutes to wedge the mysterious thing up from the floorboards, the scraping and cracking sounds as she worked causing the cat's ears to twitch. At first trying to be gentle in order not to damage it, the frustrated Agnes began striking at the edges until finally, with a grinding squeal, she pried the rock-like object from the floorboards.

She held it in one pudgy hand, observing its jagged reflective surface in the light. It was warm to the touch and incredibly light for how hard it was. Its full size was about that of a golf ball. Staring in wonder, Agnes rolled it around in her hands, marveling at its texture and its possible origin. This went on for perhaps two minutes, before there came a mechanical hissing sound, and she gasped as what felt like a needle jabbed her palm. She dropped the black thing on the floor and stared at her palm, where a black dot appeared right in the center. A small bead of blood formed there, and she pressed her hand against her robe to stop the bleeding.

She looked down and her eyes widened as she saw the thin, black protrusion jutting from the surface, a feature she swore was not there when she first picked it up. This needle like nozzle was spewing forth a steady stream of stringy black goo that collected on the carpet like ink.

"Oh my," she said and recoiled from the object. That's when she saw Buttercup leap from the stairs and run at the black thing, swatting at it with claws extended. The obsidian object skittered across the floor as Buttercup swatted it, flinging black goo across the room. The other two cats bolted from their hiding place and scattered as the black thing came towards them. Buttercup began incessantly licking the paw that she struck the object with, then limped back up the stairs, mewling painfully from the shadows.

Agnes began to feel strange. A tingling sensation that started in her stung palm began to work its way up her arm, as if the limb had fallen asleep and was just now receiving blood flow. She tried to flex her fingers, and felt the tendons grow stiff. She looked down at the black streaks that now marred the carpet, and she could swear the stains were moving. With a groan she got up, intending to look for the black thing. But suddenly she felt dizzy, her eyes feeling swollen in their sockets, her thoughts confused, sluggish.

She decided that she would deal with this mess in the morning, and if she still felt ill, she would go see Dr. Sutherland. Right now, all she could think about was laying down, being under the covers, in darkness. As dark as she could get it.

"Have you been outside the country recently, Miss Mayberry?"

"No, I haven't even left Buck's Point in years."

"Come in contact with any sick looking individuals?"

"No, unless you count those damn methheads that hang out in front of the Texaco."

"And you say you just woke up with it one day? You can't recall cutting yourself or injuring that hand somehow?" he asked.

"That's right. I just woke up with it." The questions went on for some time, before Dr. Sutherland finally sighed and examined the quarter-sized black mark on his patient's palm one more time. Agnes had fully intended on telling Dr. Sutherland about the black thing that came into her house. But on the ride out to his office, she had a sudden idea to keep the black object a secret. Paranoid thoughts of what might happen if the government or some other officials found out about her little gift from the stars floated insidiously around in her brain. These thoughts didn't entirely seem to be hers, but she knew to go with her gut, and her gut told her that she needed to proceed carefully.

The fifty-year-old doctor hadn't seen anything like it in his twenty years as a general practitioner. A scab-like growth that was completely black and sported fine downy fuzz of the same color, which had, according to his elderly patient, appeared while she was sleeping.

"And it doesn't hurt to touch?" he implored as he looked again under one of the adjustable high intensity lamps.

"No, not really."

"Well that's good at least, because I'm going to have to take a piece of this and send it off for a biopsy. I haven't seen anything like this before," he said, taking a pair of tweezers from the utilities cabinet in the corner of the examination room. He stooped over with Agnes's upturned palm held up to his face and very gently picked at the edge of the growth, intending to only take a small chunk. Instead the whole growth came off in one spongy mass as he pulled. Agnes gasped and yanked her hand away.

"Oh my goodness. I am so sorry, Miss Mayberry, I didn't mean to peel the whole thing off. Did that hurt?" he asked sheepishly. The elderly woman was looking at her hand in stunned awe.

"No. I just, I don't know. I felt *something*," she said. She sounded flustered. Dr. Sutherland quickly placed the specimen in a sterile culture container and went to examine her hand. He saw that the skin where the growth had been was pink and pale, like freshly healed scar tissue. In the center of the pink circle was a small, black spot, as if Agnes had stabbed her hand with a pencil.

"Hmmm. Could be an infection. Yet it doesn't look infected, no pus or swelling, but we won't know for sure until we get your blood tests back. In the meantime, I'm going to prescribe you an antibiotic just in case something is brewing inside we don't know about." Agnes looked up at him, her eyes wide with fear.

"*Antibiotics?*" she asked. "Is that really necessary?"

"I'm not sure yet, but it's better to be safe, than sorry. At your age Miss Mayberry, even the slightest infection could put you in great danger. I'll write you a two-week script for Amoxicillin. That should cover all our bases until I can get your blood results back and this thing tested," he said, patting the sterile container with the black growth in it. He bandaged her hand with a large band-aid that was smeared with an antibacterial ointment and sent her on her way.

Agnes's closest neighbors, the Whitakers, were a kind young couple who farmed livestock a half mile down the road from her house and were usually the ones to give her rides into the nearby town of Terrell, since her husband was taken by prostate cancer. Agnes hated to be a burden on anyone, but her eyesight and arthritis had deteriorated to the point where driving was simply not an option anymore. But it was days like today, where she felt quite peculiar and ill, that she was grateful for their support.

She was even more thankful that it was Tom driving her today and not Lucille, who was the more talkative of the two by a long shot. Agnes was not in the mood for small talk about cattle commodity prices and the future of the grain belt. As they drove along the county highway that would take them the ten miles back to Buck's Point, Agnes's mind reeled from the peculiar reactions she had in the doctor's office.

She replayed the part where the growth was taken from her body. It did not feel like the benign tingle of a peeling scab or the raw hot sensation of freshly parted flesh. When that black mold left her skin, it was like sundering some kind of umbilical cord to another entity. A profoundly disturbing loss of a vital connection. And absurdly she found herself *missing the growth.* As soon as the black stuff left her flesh, she felt an insane urge to snatch it from the steel tweezers and press it back onto her flesh. It took an alarming amount of will power not to do just that.

Then there was the matter of her response to that word. *Antibacterial.* As soon as the words left his mouth and her brain registered the meaning and implication, a brief image of multiplying amoebas being dissolved by some pharmaceutical elixir flashing across her mind, she felt ill and disgusted. It was as if her mind had formed the deepest Pavlovian aversion to that specific word, and even now she found herself involuntarily fixating on it, her mind slowly crawling over each vowel and consonant as if some new part of her consciousness was studying this word and her understanding of its definition. It made no sense, because she had taken antibiotics several times before in her life for various ailments and had never had a negative reaction to them. Yet now, she recalled those past experiences with appalled horror, the very fact she had ingested such vile nostrums made her skin crawl.

"So, he didn't prescribe you anything huh?" Tom had asked before they hit the backroads out of town, pulling into the Walgreens that they usually stopped at to refill Agnes's script for gout medication.

"Nope," she lied. "Dang doctors don't know nothing these days." She glared at the building through the thick rims of the sunglasses she wore the whole ride to and from the doctor's office, despite the day being heavily overcast.

"Oh, alright. Well, I need to go in anyway to get some coffee and things. You need anything before we head back over yonder?" he asked as he got out. Agnes was about to reply no, when she suddenly blurted out something that wasn't even on her mind.

"Beer. And bread. Three loaves of bread. Honey Wheat," she said quickly. Tom blinked, and did a double take towards the tan store.

"Uh...Agnes, not one to tell you how to live your life, but I thought you couldn't drink beer. Flairs up your gout, you know, and –"

"Just get it," she said. Her hands fumbled around seemingly of their own volition as she reached for her purse. She pulled out a twenty and handed it to him. He took the money, looking at it with confused eyes.

"Well, alright. What kind of beer you want, Miss Mayberry?" At this she was silent for a moment, her mind quickly racing through the catalog of beer brands she had encountered in her lifetime.

"Uhm... Pabst. Or Budweiser. Whichever is cheaper. As much as you can buy with the money left over from the three loaves."

While Tom went to fetch the items, Agnes gingerly peeled up the band-aid that covered her wound, eager to be rid of the bandage and the foul ointment that ignorant man who had apparently been her doctor for ten years had administered. She smiled with relief when she saw the thin black film was already blossoming out from the center of the puncture site. She wadded up the bandage and threw it out the passenger window, glad to be gone of it.

She kept her hands clasped together as they rode back to her house, a twelve pack of beer and three loaves of Bunny bread between her ankles. She had much rest and consuming to do.

IT HAD BEEN a week since the black object came hurtling into Agnes's home, a home whose interior was now almost unrecognizable from its previous state. The living room, once filled with shelves of her collections of commemorative plates and pictures of her family, was now being slowly transformed into some kind of make-shift green house. After coming back from her trip into town, she immediately began work on this project that she did not comprehend. After rummaging around the entire house, not really knowing or understanding what she was searching for, Agnes came upon the old four-person Ozark Trail tent Bernard kept in the garage, a tent they had camped in quite a bit back when they were middle-aged and more adventurous, before the gout had virtually crippled her. She took this and set it up in the middle of the living room.

Once this was done, she went back into the garage and found four of the heavy-duty tarps they had bought back when the '98 Tornado rolled through Buck's Point and took most of the Mayberry's shingles with it. She draped these over the tent, and secured them together with a roll of duct tape. She made sure to leave a small opening in the bottom that she could crawl into. She did all this on her normally agonized feet, which were now mercifully numb as something blocked her brain from registering the pain signals from her screaming nerve endings.

Misty and Patty watched their owner's bizarre burst of energy with great agitation. The two cats were growing hungry and thirsty, and did not understand why Agnes, in her new co-opted state, had forgotten all about them. They did not want to go near her though, now that she reeked of the foul molding decay that had entered the house so abruptly. The felines could sense the energy coming from the object, which was stuck in one corner of the kitchen, blossoming out its black presence. Somewhere in that pulsating dark shadow was

Buttercup, who had come down from her hiding spot in Agnes's bedroom to be one with the growth in the corner. The cat was now totally covered in the black growth, the whole mass contracting and expanding subtly with its breathing.

In her singular purpose to construct the bizarre structure, Agnes had left the back door open when she went to gather great handfuls of dirt and grass from the yard with which to spread across the floor of the tent. The cats, thoroughly disturbed by the aberration in their once comfy home, raced out of the open doorway, escaping the madness.

Once the structure was complete, Agnes brought in her food from Walgreens, as well as everything she could find in her pantry or refrigerator that was rich in carbs and yeast. She ate bread and drank some of her beer as she did this, her normally hearty appetite increased to a nearly ravenous magnitude, her body seemingly starving for carbs. Despite the fact she hardly ever touched alcohol as a preventative measure of flaring up the gout, she barely felt a buzz as empty cans piled up around the tent. It was if her body was using up the sustenance as soon as it entered her GI tract.

With what she came to think of as *the incubator* now fully stocked with bread, various leftovers from the refrigerator, a bag of cat food, and six rotten, moldy potatoes she had forgotten about that were festering in the back of her dry goods cabinet (her mouth watered at the site and smell of those in particular), she went to shut all the drapes in the house. Once it was as dark as she could get it, she turned off the A/C, hoping the ninety-degree days they were having would transform the house into the appropriate climate quickly.

"That's right, Buttercup, things will be just right soon," she said in a voice that sounded more like the vocalizations of a bullfrog than that of a human timbre. Although she hadn't seen Buttercup all week, she knew the cat was alive somewhere close, due to the extrasensory network of connections she had formed thanks to the mold, which now covered her whole right arm and blossomed onto part of her chest. Everything it touched she was aware of. It was a rather jarring sensation, like being in ten places at once, but she acclimated.

At least, part of her did. The other part, the original consciousness of Agnes Mayberry, was slowly shrinking, the ever-growing alien sentience crowding out her thought processes and cognitive awareness. It was like being robbed of your own brain one sense at a time. Somewhere, in a dark, untouched corner of her occipital lobe, the remainder of Agnes Mayberry screamed a silent cry of helplessness as her hijacked body retreated into the dark, fetid incubator this new consciousness had created for itself.

"Tom, I really think you should go over there. It's been two weeks since we've heard from her. You know how she is; every other day she gives one of us a ring for something," Lucille said after trying for the fifth time to contact their elderly neighbor. They both had been sitting in the living room, watching the special news report on the growing quarantine zone around the Mississippi River towards Saint Louis, when Lucille checked her phone and realized the absence of Miss Mayberry's sometimes incessant phone calls.

"Oh, you're just riled up Luce. Seeing all this news talk about toxic algae blooms and pandemics just got you anxious, as was the intended effect, I'm sure. You know how the news likes to scare people. Agnes is a tough old girl," Tom said distractedly as his eyes stared at his laptop. Someone on Facebook had shared what was an apparently leaked aerial footage from a surveillance drone of a forest in Alabama that was completely covered in a black, membranous material. This infestation had apparently begun after last week's surprise meteor shower that had astronomers and geophysicists scratching their heads. He had no idea what the hell was going on up north with the river, but this looked like something out of a Lovecraftian nightmare. He quickly closed out of the video as his wife walked over, not wanting to scare her further.

"Please honey, do it for me," she said, putting a hand on his shoulder. He really, *really* didn't want to go out there. Agnes had been acting incredibly weird on the ride back to town. He didn't tell Luce about her almost robotic commands for booze and bread. Or the black spot he saw on her hand as she was grabbing her groceries.

"Alright, fine, I'll go," he lied, intending instead to head out to The Big Muddy Bar and Grill to grab a few drinks with Roscoe and Dave, and pick their brains about the weird stories they were hearing from Saint Louis, and the long, black streamers that were often seen floating down the river.

"Thank you. I'll ride with you," she said, kissing him on the cheek as he repressed a pained sigh.

It only took four minutes to get to Agnes's, and in that short stretch of time Tom's apprehension towards the woman and her general vicinity grew substantially. As he drove up the winding driveway, he noticed the hole in the side of her house. It looked like someone had shot a ten gauge deer slug through the wall. As they pulled up next to the scabrous old Buick that hadn't been driven in years, Tom could see with some alarm that the windows were square voids absent of any light, or...*anything*. It was like they were painted black.

He parked the truck and got out. The first thing they noticed was the smell. The high, sweet tang of spoiled fruit and moldy bread mixed with a muskier, heavy undertone.

"Jesus, do you smell that?" Luce said, putting a hand to her nose and mouth.

"Hon... I really think we should go. We can call Sheriff Jones and get him to do a welfare check or something," he said, almost gagging as he talked. Then something very peculiar began to happen. The sense of growing dread had been replaced by an unexplainable pull towards the house. He could feel an insatiable curiosity steal over him as the smell transformed from something rank to something quite pleasing, like freshly baked banana bread.

"Tom...I feel weird... I really think we should go check on her," she said in a voice that was tranquil and sleepy. She walked unevenly around to the front door, and Tom saw her eyes were dilated wide, looking like she was flying high on LSD or something. A part of him knew what was going on was profoundly wrong, and that they should leave immediately. But another part of him wanted to give in to the warm, calming feelings that seemed to come from absolutely nowhere.

He followed his wife towards the door, the smell becoming even stronger, like he was in a bakery full of freshly baked sweet bread. As they drew closer to the door, the pull was almost unbearable, like they had powerful magnets embedded in their brains, the house being the metal bar that pulled them in.

Lucille went first. She didn't even knock. The door didn't open at first, but she shoved with her shoulder, and with a great liquid moving sound, like someone stirring a huge bowl of wet pasta, she entered the obsidian void. For a brief moment the overwhelming miasma of human waste hit their noses, before this turned into something savory like beef stew. She walked into a yielding, black mass that stuck to her skin as she encountered it. A warm, black pillow that filled her mouth, nose, and ears. Tom followed shortly after, nearly throwing himself at the stuff in eagerness to be in contact with it.

The obsidian mass consumed them, and they gladly succumbed.

6

RED DEATH

"Holy shit," Lana Briggs said in stunned amazement. "Mitch, get your ass over here, I think we just hit the jack pot!" Mitch Connell, her shipmate, floated over from the refinement station he was at, processing the last of the small bits of precious metals they got from their previous salvage trip. They both stood peering over the LCD screen showing the dark vessel floating through the cluttered debris of ancient wreckage. Mitch studied the markings on the large ship closely and noted the display read *Ship Class: E-18 mobile excavation and drill series* in the classification bracket where the probe ran diagnostics on the derelict vessel. Realizing he was looking at an old school Russian research ship, Mitch lit up with excitement and clapped Lana on the back.

"We sure as hell did hit the jackpot. That there is an old-ass Sokolov digger, made back before they had nanocomposite metals to make ships ultra-light. That metal beast is built like a tank and probably has enough raw titanium ore and gold plating to totally clean out the scrap yard appraisers. If we manage to strip her down and haul it back with us we will be made for at least eight or nine months minimum. What's the status on the ship dexterity? Is it boardable?"

"Diagnostics show some slight hull damage, probably from a stray impact, and a small tear on the starboard side, but the room it's in looks to be sealed off. Structural integrity of the docking bay is 95 percent, so we should be good to go," she said, sounding giddy.

"Excellent, because I need to see just how many goodies are onboard and check the black box. That thing looks like it's been floating around a couple hundred years and we're gonna need the flight recorder to give to the claims agency in case there's cold ones aboard, which is a possibility as you well know. I'll go prep the scout and get suited up. See you down there," the large man said and floated down the hallway, his bulk making his journey awkward.

Lana, who was much smaller and dexterous than Mitch, easily caught up to him as she soared through the hallway and rounded the corner to where the small two-person intercept craft was waiting for them.

MUCH LIKE THE planets they had inhabited, the early years of human space exploration always left trails of litter and pollution in their wake as the species slowly refined their crude methods of transporting goods across the stars. As technology improved, older obsolete ships and stations were simply left to drift in the heavens, occasionally falling into a planet's orbit and becoming a problem if the planet was inhabited. Sometimes ships were abandoned because of crew expiration, as many early journeys into deep space were fatal due to ill preparation, poorly built jump drives and the ignorance of worm hole travel at the time.

This created a booming business among what the colonies had termed "junk pirating," where skilled pilots with strong stomachs, a lot of spare time, and extensive knowledge in the raw materials market would build scavenger ships to intercept these discarded monuments to human engineering, technological progress allowing them to make big money on mankind's failings and occasionally get rewarded for helping identify pilots who were MIA.

However, as the years bore on and humans progressed in their technologies and knowledge of the stars, the number of ghost ships and easily accessible material caches decreased to the point where junkers such as Mitch and Lana were having to scour ever deeper into the edge of their home solar system to hit pay dirt. The old Russian digger was a needle in a very, very large haystack, and Lana had wondered on the statistical luck they must have had to stumble upon it this far outside the Milky Way. She knew that geological teams were sent out on daring expeditions long ago to find intelligent life on the other side of the solar system, with many of them never returning due to the primitive, shoddily built jump drives, which the research vessels were the first to get as desperate scientists kept exploring deeper, desperate to find new life and new planets to call home.

However, some of those ancient ships were brought back into accessible traffic areas as the natural inertia of their trajectory altered due to planetary perturbations, occasionally spitting the forgotten ships back towards populated areas of space over many light years. That must have been the case for the E18, as its maiden launch date appeared to have been over three hundred years ago. It was as much a historical artifact as it was a goldmine of raw resources.

Yet as they drew closer to the ship, excitement turned to anxiousness, as it always did when they were getting ready to board. Mitch and Lana had been on over forty salvage runs together since opening up shop five years ago, and there was simply no way of telling what you were going to float into when you forced open the bay doors into a dark intergalactic tomb. Lana and Mitch had both seen their share of corpses, whose remains were always perfectly preserved and freeze-dried in the oxygen deprived vacuum of space. That was until you jumpstarted the engine and the artificial environment kicked in, where upon the corpses, which had sometimes been dead for over a hundred years, would begin to rapidly putrefy into a terrible smelling goop in their EVO suits. That was the ethically tricky part of the job, trying to locate and respectfully dispose of the human remains before you got the power turned back on. They had both learned that lesson the hard and disgusting way, and made sure never to repeat such mistakes.

Keeping this in mind, Lana mentally prepared herself for whatever it was that lay beyond the blast bay doors. It could be totally empty or they could find mutilated bodies from the occasional space fever making ill selected crew members go crazy and do terrible things. She tried to keep her mind off those grisly memories though as they decelerated and approached the tubular receptacle of the docking bay.

"I'll take care of the doors. You ready to breach?" Mitch asked, but Lana was already depressurizing the small cockpit and preparing to pop the windshield. It was a solid routine they had down pat by now, and muscle memory took over easily. Mitch would get out, float his way around to the small exterior terminal override panel found on the side of every standard federation ship, disengage the magnetic locks and then pry open the doors with a magnetic winch, something he was suited for given his brute strength, and then Lana would gently glide the scout through the narrow gap and bingo, they were in. Find any human remains, relieve them of their ID chips for the database and catapult them out into space or use the ship's incinerator if it had one. Take inventory, fire up the ship, and pilot it back to their massive towing station, or if the ship wasn't operable, they would take the towing station to it. Just another job.

Except it didn't feel that way; not this time. The interior of the docking bay seemed especially foreboding as the small observation light at the front of the scout illuminated a catastrophic mess of floating debris. Smashed and mangled bits of electronics and cables mostly. Lana could see the broken windows of the boarding terminal. She could also see her first body floating serenely amidst the levitating chaos as the magnetic receptors on the scout clanked firmly to the metal runway. The corpse's back was to her, but she noticed with a sinking heart how small it was. *Oh god, don't let it be a child,* she thought to herself. She tried to tell herself it was just more worksite jitters, which she got occasionally. But this wasn't just excited anticipation. Something felt wrong here, but she couldn't explain what. Despite this, she kept her mouth shut. Mitch was a respectful coworker, but any sign of feminine distress on the job was usually enough to put him in a patronizing *are you sure you're cut out for this kinda work?* attitude that she absolutely hated. She nonchalantly gave Mitch the thumbs up as he successfully navigated through the maelstrom of junk.

"Jesus, those Ruskies must have had one hell of a rowdy party in here before they shut down," Mitch said through her earpiece, marveling at the scope of random destruction.

"Yeah, also there's a cold one to the north of you. I spotted it coming in. I'm guessing we're gonna have more remains aboard. Let's just focus on getting the bodies rounded up so we can get the lights on," she said, trying not to let the anxiousness come through in her voice. She wanted more than anything for the juice to be on right now. Most ghost ships were dark in principle, but at least with a run close to orbit they could get some backlight in through observation windows of the ship to go with their flashlights. But they were on the dark side of Orion, and there were zero windows on the ship, save for the captain's bridge. The darkness in here seemed to hold physical weight it was so dense, as if she could almost feel its mass pressing in at the narrow cone of light her flashlight emitted, eager to snuff out any and all illumination.

She was getting ready to approach the corpse she saw on the way in and search the flight suit for ID, but she paused for a moment to look to the eastern wall by the entrance to the terminal. Her flashlight shown a bright red message spray-painted in Russian on it. The words were quick and jagged, their foreign symbols appearing scribed by a frantic hand.

"Hey, Mitch? Can you read Russian?" she asked, pointing towards the graffiti.

Mitch grabbed onto one of the handrails to stop his motion and studied the words. "Hmmm... nope. But I can snap a picture and send it to the worthless ship AI we have and see if it can translate it for us." He did so with the helmet mounted camera he had on, which also ran real time biomonitoring stats and live feed to their salvage ship an uncomfortable distance away. "Artemis, can you photo analyze the text in the picture I just sent you into English please?"

"Pr..r…rocessing r…reque…que…uest," a glitchy female voice told them through their suit intercoms.

"I'm sure you are, worthless cheap bitch. Don't get your hopes up with her," he begrudgingly told Lana. "Knew I shoulda nutted up the extra forty grand for the Athena series."

Mitch continued on ahead, sweeping the area with his flashlight while Lana approached the corpse. She slowly turned it over and saw with frightened bewilderment the flight suit seemed to lose its shape as she spun it around. As she got a glimpse into the helmet of the deceased she reared back in surprise. Instead of the usual pale, bloated face of a vacuumed corpse there was only the shrunken, shriveled face of someone of unidentifiable gender. The skin was slowly flaking away like ash inside the helmet, and the eyes, no more than small dehydrated gray raisins, rolled around crudely in the cavernous sockets. The hair which was short and cropped, was an ashen gray, as if something had sucked every ounce of color and life from this person.

"Mitch, come back here and take a look at this," she said, unable to hide the tremble in her voice. She mentally cursed herself for letting this benign peculiarity spook her.

But Mitch was nowhere to be seen, and for a moment she panicked as she couldn't find him or hear a response. Then she heard his thick husky voice, but with his own small flavor of fear in it. She couldn't think of a time where she had ever heard Mitch Connell sound afraid in her life.

"What… the… fuck," he said slowly, and she assumed he had discovered his own corpse in the bizarre mummified condition, or worse.

"Mitch? Where are you?" she asked, pushing off a wall and towards his last seen location.

"Down the hall and to the left. I just found someone but they're… they're… I don't know. There's nothing to him but skin and bones, and not even that. I can feel him falling apart in his suit," he said, revulsion thick in his voice.

She frantically scrambled around the corner, losing her grip in the zero gravity and almost crashing into him as she rounded the corner.

"Jesus, watch out!" he yelled.

"Sorry!" she said, and observed the corpse Mitch held. "I found one just like that in the docking bay. Whatever happened to them occurred before the ship depressurized. You wouldn't see this kind of decay unless the corpses were over a thousand years old. But we were still a one planet species back then," She said, desperately trying to rack her brain for some logical reason as to the corpses' extremely weathered state.

"What the hell could have caused this? It looks like someone hooked them up to a shop vac and damn near drained them of... well... *everything*. I've never seen anything like this." There was a momentary uncomfortable silence as they stared at the husk of cosmonaut.

Finally, Lana spoke, abandoning her tough girl act as she saw she wasn't the only one thoroughly creeped out.

"I don't like this, Mitch. I know this place is a gold mine but... Jesus. What happened to these guys?" she asked more to herself than to him.

"Your guess is as good as mine. Let's press on. I got the blueprints loaded in. This place gives me the creeps too, but we came here for a reason. We both got loans to pay back and stomachs to feed. If we hadn't stumbled upon this ship we would be screwed. Let's get the bodies accounted for, and I'm sure we will find a simple answer to this soon enough. Let's not split up though, this place is big and I don't wanna have to hunt you down. I know that's gonna take longer but... something doesn't feel right here." Lana had no qualms with sticking together, the thought of navigating these long-abandoned halls alone gave her a chill. Reluctantly, they plunged into the bowels of the ship.

They scoured the first two levels in the dark save for their flashlight beams, where they navigated long, cramped corridors filled with random debris and the occasional floating corpse, each one in that same diminished state. Every corner they rounded was a test in self-discipline to confront the adjacent corridor, but slowly and painstakingly they corralled all the corpses they could find and tied them up using some rope they found, though by the time they had gotten the bodies back to the flight deck they had basically disintegrated to dust in their suits. When they got to the third level of the ship they had close to ten bodies, if you could call them that, and were coming up on their eleventh casualty when Mitch stopped and shined his light at a hallway legend, all in Russian.

"Hey, I think this might be the generator room. I recognize that symbol, universal for jump drive. Let me see if I can at least get the lights going without turning on the oxygen pumps so we can speed this up a bit," he said and they headed down a T shaped junction where they proceeded left. They entered a huge room where the large turbines and encased coils of the engine and jump drive were. Mitch did a quick shine over of the hardware and determined it all looked in good shape, despite being archaic engine models. Then he found the small circular console in the center of the room and plugged his HUD into it, where he was then able to jumpstart the console online using his suit's power pack.

"Now, let's see if I can find an English menu on this son of a bitch," he said, fiddling with menu screens. While he did this Lana explored cautiously, shining her light around and observing the peculiar pattern of cracks she had noticed around the rest of the ship. Strange long black crevices that went up the walls and sometimes scaled around equipment, as if some massive corrosive laser had seared a path erratically around the interior of the ship.

She was floating up to one sharp column of the black line, noticing up close it wasn't a crack; it looked more like blackened ice, with a sort of reflective, organic surface, almost like flattened or dehydrated tree roots. She was only inches from it, studying it intently when Mitch yelled:

"Aha! Mitch the genius, how does he do it?" A few seconds later Lana shielded her eyes as harsh, white light filled her world. Her eyes adjusted, and she exhaled an amazed breath as she took in the real dimensions of the room and ship, which now felt much bigger. She also got a better look at the black... *stuff* that was laced all over the room, with one narrow tendril reaching on the floor right up to the console Mitch was standing at. It seemed to be concentrated here in the engine room, at least compared to its traces in the rest of the ship she had seen. "All right, lets hustle and gather up the rest of the bodies now that we can actually see what the hell we are doing. I can only run the auxiliary power cell for fifteen minutes before we run out of enough juice to crank the engines, so let's not waste any time, come on," Mitch said, and Lana followed her partner down the final two levels where the cafeteria and laboratory were.

The cafeteria and crew's quarters surprisingly didn't have any bodies, just a lot of floating kitchen ware riff raff, although Lana took note of a few floating butcher knives that had what appeared to be dried blood crusted on their blades.

They descended to the bottom level, the laboratory, which featured several partitioned-off glass rooms with various geological instruments floating around inside. A large digging rover was chained down next to a few other transport rovers, and Lana could see that whatever the black crusty stuff was had almost completely covered the digging rover, giving it a vague shadow quality, as if it had originated and then grew from the vehicle. Over to the far corner they could see where the wall had imploded outwards and they were afforded a jagged view of space.

"Found our hull breach. Looks like it was self-contained though. Interesting," Mitch said nonchalantly.

"I keep seeing all this tar like crap around. What is it you think?" Lana asked, pointing to the black crust-encased rover. The crust seemed to cover the outer edges of the tear where the metal had ballooned out, almost as if it were there to seal it shut, which it almost did.

"Could be chemical flame retardant that was sprayed and then frozen after the power went off. Or busted cooling pipes leaking god knows what and freezing solid. Who knows, who cares. No bodies down here, let's head back." They did, making their way back up to the flight deck and corralling the tethered group of suited dust bunnies out the pried open launch bay doors and giving them a shove out to into space. Lana then put the acquired ID bio-tags into a pocket in her space suit and they headed back down to the engine room.

They cleared the area around the console as best they could of debris so as not to be injured by falling material, and then braced themselves for the jarring crash as gravity and artificial atmosphere kicked on and everything floating in the ship came crashing back down. She felt the vibrating of the huge engines start to fire up, and then a hard pulling sensation followed by a thunderous thud as a whole E class ship worth of random derelict crap fell to the floor, and gravity reoriented their bodies, a disorienting sensation.

"Oxygen level reading 0% percent. Beginning air cycle," an automated voice told them in English. Lana didn't know how Mitch pulled it off, but somehow he'd gotten the ship's AI to switch from Russian to English. He could be an asshole, but he was a whiz mechanic asshole.

"Should be able to un-suit in about ten minutes. May as well get comfortable while we pilot this beast back to the ship. I'm gonna see if I can do a rollback on the pilot's log and figure out what the hell happened to these guys," Mitch said and began exploring the ship's information terminal diligently.

While he was focused on that, Lana went back to staring at the blackened trails of chemical fluid or whatever it was. It looked slightly different than it did a minute ago, but she couldn't put her finger on what it was. Five minutes of silence passed.

"Oxygen levels at 50%. Approaching stasis," the voice chirped from the ship's sound system.

Then Lana realized what it was. The black stuff was changing color. Slowly, almost imperceptibly, she saw the glossy black crust begin to slowly bloom into a dark violet, and then from a dark violet into...

"Hey, Lana? You should come look at this. I can't make any sense of it. Maybe the translator on this behemoth is busted or something"

Lana walked over, suddenly feeling a strong tension build around her, as if they were coming to the precipice of some horrible realization.

She glanced down at the rectangular terminal screen and read the captain's log, which was dated July 8, 2125, over a hundred years ago.

WE HAVE CALLED IT RED DEATH
IT IS SENTIENT
HOME ORIGIN IS EUROPA
THE SHIP MUST BE CLEANSED
OXYGEN MUST REMAIN AT 0%
DO NOT COME FIND US, IGNORE DISTRESS BEACONS
BEWARE THE RED DEATH
IT MUST NOT BREATHE
OXYGEN BRINGS DEATH

They stared at the bizarre log for a minute or so before the onboard AI chirped back in and snapped them out of their contemplation. "Oxygen levels at 85%. Hull breach detected in research engineering sublevel A. Obstruction detected in flight bay. Unable to proceed. Stand by."

"I don't get it. The last captain's log sign-in before this shit was two weeks prior, and the captain seemed excited. Apparently, they just left some ice titan moon with soil samples they were going ape shit over, literally a ship full of nerds just drooling over—"

But Mitch was cut off as Artemis chimed in "Te...Te...text encryption analys...sis c...c...complete. Message rel-rel-relay sent to your h...hud..." and suddenly their screen visors were filled with generated computer text which read:

DO NOT TRY AND SAVE US
IGNORE ALL DISTRESS BEACONS
RED DEATH MUST DIE
SHIP MUST BE CLEANSED

OXYGEN BRINGS DEATH

Suddenly Lana felt an overwhelming dread fill her. "Shut it off, the oxygen. *Now*. I don't know what the hell Red Death is but clearly these guys didn't want the place back up and running," She said. Then she looked around and was horrified at what she saw. The black-turning-purple veins that coated the hallways was now a deep blood red, and they were *moving*. Pulsating and slowly spreading, growing along the walls like rapidly growing tree roots. "Mitch, let's get the fuck out of here! Shut that shit off and—"

But there was a scream and a loud slurping sound that interrupted her and she looked back towards the console.

Mitch had been standing on a patch of the previously innate material when he was accessing the terminal, not giving the stuff much attention in his always rational mind. But now the reanimated viscera had completely engulfed the leg of his space suit, and was making its way up his torso, with one silk thin tendril racing up towards his helmet, lining itself along the thin seal of his helmet baffle and somehow penetrating into it. He flailed and screamed, but was unable to move as his left foot was now firmly rooted to the metallic floor.

"MITCH! HOLY SHIT!" Lana screamed, trying to pull the growing veins of alien life off him. But they did not tear or give, simply elongating like warm toffee as she pulled and pulled, until she herself was covered in thin writhing strands of the stuff. OXYGEN BRINGS DEATH was burned into her mind, and in the chaos she managed to bend over the console and try to shut off the power, but the roots of the red abomination had begun webbing itself around the touch screen, obstructing her from inputting any kind of command as if it sensed what she was trying to do.

"R...R...runnnn!" a thin voice emanated from her suit intercom, and she looked over in horror to see that Mitch, a man larger than life and built like a bull, was slowly diminishing in size in his suit, the thin veins of alien life burrowing itself into his ears and nose, pulsating and throbbing as it drank greedily from the man's essence. His once broad stone slab face was now gaunt and emaciated, and his whole body twitched and trembled as the thing feasted.

Lana ran, sprinting with all her might down the narrow corridors, claustrophobia and blind terror coalescing into a maddening energy that sent her rocketing through the ship. The thin strands that had engulfed her when trying to free Mitch finally reached their stretched limit and let loose with wet tendon-like snapping sounds as she exited the room. All around her, the once blackened crust was plumping up and turning red, like some corrupted rose bloom, and the veiny strands reached greedily out towards her as she vaulted up the stairways towards her scout. *It was simply waiting for someone to thaw it* she thought frantically as the mysterious cryptic messages left by the Russian research team now made terrible sense.

She made her way towards the flight deck, hyperventilating, leg muscles burning from running in her heavy suit. She stole one look back before entering the hangar and saw that the entire corridor was webbed in a mass of pulsating red. She took a deep breath and tried to steady herself. She had a good forty feet on the growing mass but it was gaining quickly. She started climbing over the fallen debris towards the scout when she saw with sinking terror that the blast bay doors were shut, the pneumatic winch laying pinched between the two massive doors like a flattened accordion as the power had enforced an automatic reset. "No, no, no!" she screamed, looking around frantically.

She climbed on top of a mound of junk and tried to look for the small circular portholes that meant an emergency life pod station. She wondered if they even had life pods on ships this old, and it didn't help that all the damn labels were Russian. She scrambled around, scanning the walls, looking back towards the terminal door, seeing that the red roots were now at the edge of the doorway and spreading.

She ran along one wall until she found what she was looking for: twelve rows of circular portholes, the red ejection lights above them lit up on all but one, at the far end closest to the terminal doorway. She sprinted for it and slammed the green button that she assumed was an open button. The small circular porthole slid away with agonizing slowness, and she could see the human-sized pneumatic tube slowly being elevated for entry. "Come the fuck onnnnnnnnnn!" she moaned, slamming on the wall trying to will the life pod to go faster.

The growth was in the room now, rapidly blossoming on the high walls in great spider web shapes, with one fat straight vein growing slowly but steadily towards her, like a gesturing finger eager to devour. It was halfway across the hanger, snaking around debris and closing to one hundred feet. Then fifty feet, picking up speed as if it sensed her near escape.

There was a cheery sounding chime as the life pod was locked into the launch tube and the clear pod door opened. A pleasant-sounding woman's voice spoke to her in Russian, probably telling her the tube was ready and to please enter calmly. She ignored it as she grabbed onto the handrail above the porthole and slid her way into the tube right as the tendrils were about to close in on her foot, immediately closing the small porthole behind her. She didn't notice the small strand that clung to her boot. She strapped herself in and hit the green launch button that hung over her head on a small panel. She watched as the exterior bay door for the tube slid slowly open, yellow caution lights swirling in the narrow metal launch corridor. She looked up and saw that the metal bulkhead was bulging in as the focused mass of alien growth pushed against it.

Finally, she saw the circular porthole into the abyss, and hit the launch button again right as the reception door caved in. There was a great pushing sensation as the torpedo shot itself away from the ship, G forces slamming her into the seat. She looked up in time to see a blossoming veiny mass of the growth get ripped out into space from explosive decompression, and it began slowly withering back into the black crust.

Lana sobbed hysterically in her helmet as her brain tried to process what just happened, understanding that a man she once thought invincible was now a withered ghost, understanding that she had just encountered the first known instance of extraterrestrial life in human history. She cried hard for perhaps ten minutes while the pod soared through space, waiting for her to engage the rescue beacon. As she pulled herself together, she reached blindly through tear-streaked eyes and hit the toggle, which would alert any ship within two hundred thousand miles of her location. Then she looked down as she felt a peculiar tingling sensation in her foot, and saw the red mass blooming.

7

SEARCH AND DESTROY

THEIR EYES WERE ALL HAUNTED. I could see it plainly on their stone faces as the swift boat ferried us up the Mekong, away from that terrible place where I saw men, women, and children become something unspeakable. Not even the occasional *pang* of a ricochet from the VC as they took pot shots at us from the bank could stir my men from their internal traumas. I knew they were still back at Qui Nang, still trying to replay exactly what happened, trying to understand exactly what had caused them to snap like that. I was right there with them, replaying and ruminating the horrible night in my head. But I was the platoon leader. I had to show some semblance of integrity and sanity. Yet I could think of nothing to say.

It's been three weeks since the massacre, the ones the newspapers got ahold of and ripped us apart for. It's been one week since the *other* massacre, the one that's currently being spun off by the media as an ambush on a firebase. An ambush where not a single shot was fired, but twenty men, those same men whose granite faces and broken souls I looked into on that fateful day, were killed in their sleep. I am the only witness to that night, the only one that saw what became of those men, which is why I am writing this. Soon, I will have to give a sworn deposition to the events that transpired. My sanity and service to this country will fall under great speculation. I will be raked through the coals, as will the legacy of the men I led. I honestly do not know if I can get up on the stand and recall those strange and horrifying events without losing my composure.

So instead, I am here, in my lieutenant's quarters, a glorified tent, at Firebase Bravo, under supervised watch by three privates until the airfield just north of us is cleared, so that I may be flown back home to stand trial. They say that in three days, the VC should be driven out, but I am not so sure I will survive that long. It seems great, esoteric forces are at work here, with death actively hunting me, seeking me out. The question now is whether dying in this jungle would be more of a mercy than returning home, to a land that has betrayed and forsaken me.

Let it be known that everything written here is the honest and coherent testimony of captain Arnold Mattias, 102nd Strike Team Division. Written November 7, 1969.

My men and I were part of the many elite covert ops units sent out into the deepest, most unforgiving parts of South Vietnam to conduct search and destroy missions on hidden Vietcong encampments. All of the men in my company were seasoned, at least six or seven raids under all their belts, body counts for each one going up in the dozens. We were an old platoon, with a new route. After the Tet Offensive, everything changed, and there was a new, fervent push by Westmoreland and the other orchestrators to "break the enemies' resolve." Which is where we came in.

By the time we reached Qui Nang, we were exhausted, men operating on hair-trigger nerves, many of them either high or coming down from the momentary bliss of opium, which was cheap and in plentiful supply along our patrol routes. It was a three-day, rain-soaked hell march through some of the thickest jungles I'd ever encountered in the campaign. It was the height of monsoon season, and we were all soaking wet from the time we got off the boat and into the woods. We had gotten lost from bad intel, and on top of it, we had landmines to look out for, somehow without a sweeper. We were not in any shape to do patrols, but we didn't have any choice. Brass wanted intel that would lead to vast destruction of enemy matériel and a much bigger body count, no matter the cost. Which is why when we entered the small, isolated village, where we encountered the hysterical woman ranting about nonsense, we were all immediately on guard, paranoid, our judgement ill from days in the bush without rest.

My interpreter, a South Vietnamese soldier named Lu Hong, listened raptly to the frightened woman as she rambled on, while the twenty or so dog-tired husks of men and I scanned the small village with shrewd, tired eyes, looking for any and all signs of VC occupation or activity. Villagers peeked their heads out to look at these strange, pale, wraith-like men in fear and confusion, as the few children caught playing in the rain were yanked back into their homes and hushed. It was clear they didn't want us there, and the feeling was mutual. But we had a job to do, and I was going to do it to the best of my abilities.

"She says... she says that there is no Vietcong occupation here, but that, well... there's something else," Lu said quietly, not wanting the other soldiers to overhear. "Something about a VC general who is part of some kind of... sect religion. I am not even sure what exact word to use. This general sent a shaman down and placed a curse on the village. They do not have the manpower to occupy all the far eastern villages. She says there are spirits in the trees, put there by the shaman as sentries, watching us as we speak. The land here is cursed, the spirits are part of it. Any sign of betrayal by the villagers and the shaman's curse will kill everyone. Something about...demons? Or monsters. She's begging us to leave, captain. She says our presence here upsets *them* greatly...The demon spirits, I mean." I vividly remember my reaction, how I laughed out loud, a horrible, unhinged sound. I couldn't believe it.

"You gotta be fuckin' kidding me. I thought I had heard it all until now," I announced, and then instructed Lu to go through the usual *flip script*, in my naivete. I thought perhaps the old methods of persuasion would work up in this high, forbidding place, where the pervasive onslaught of modern westernism was staunchly kept at bay.

My usual area of operations for most of the campaign was down south, toward Saigon, where the people were more modernized and sympathetic to the US occupation. There, things were easier. It was clear when a village had VC in it, or that the VC was vetting the area for operations. Villagers were scared, timid. But they still believed we would beat back their enemies and help them. Usually plying the village elders with promises of food security and constant patrols to keep them safe was enough for one of them to point a gnarled finger or flip up a trapdoor, or point on a map. It also didn't hurt that the VC down there were clumsy, uncoordinated new recruits who had not quite perfected the shoot-and-poof guerrilla tactics that would later plague us like locusts. A quick call and a few napalm baths later, a contested area would be secured, body count taken, and back to base before sundown for filet mignon and half-melted M&Ms.

It was very different in Qui Nang province however. Our insertion point was ten miles east of the Cambodian border and our patrol route some hundred miles from the nearest firebase. We were *way* out in the bush, the farthest up the Mekong any S&D teams ever dared venture. Our goal was to sniff out one of the main transport hubs along the Ho Chi Minh trail and paint those sites for bombers to come in, as the generals were eager to finally shut down at least one of the routes. Unlike in the southern regions, where the civilians learned to trust us, up here in the mountainous villages, in the enemy's backyard, the white men in green uniforms were usually a harbinger of death. The rules were different in this part of the country, where the VC had many loyal followers. Trying to identify friend from foe up here was very hard, because traitors were dealt with very, *very* harshly. So, when the flip script didn't work, I had to improvise, to strategize, which, given my fatigued and nearly delirious mind, was not easy.

Although I had achieved my rank as captain through sheer luck and simply staying alive through some of the bloodiest campaigns of the war, and seeing through the red in times of chaos, I am only a man, and as such I am not infallible, and my decisions are not always the correct ones. All I knew in that moment was that my men and I were walking corpses, dead tired. We had stayed in the bush for three days, sleep a foreign concept as we blundered our way through hostile hillsides and unforgiving terrain and flooded marshes, operating on sheer faith that we didn't walk right into an ambush. Although drug use is totally forbidden in the US Army and I myself having never touched the stuff, I did not reprimand the soldiers I saw puffing on cannabis and opium joints. It was pure misery and hell I was asking those boys to go through, with none of the usual back-up or support we were used to, and I wasn't going to take away the small escapes the narcotics granted them.

By the time we reached Qui Nang, it was approaching dark. I had to have a report wired through the radio in forty-eight hours confirming our position if we wanted to call in air strikes or have any kind of air support. I had to get my men out of the elements soon. They were tough as premium leather, but every mortal man has a breaking point, and rain, heat, hordes of biting insects, and the constant threat of death can make cracks appear in the hardiest of men. It looked like we were going to have to set up shop in the village, which I was sure no one, including my own men, wanted. I ordered three teams to sweep the area, checking huts and nearby crops for any sign of insurgent activity and for a possible place to set up a temporary camp. I had Lu go around canvassing the village for signs of a hierarchy, a village elder we could bargain with. But it soon became apparent that no one was going to talk or trade.

AFTER A TENSE FOUR hours of reconnaissance and exploring, Cuningham, our medic, a wiry Bostonian with nerves of steel and ginger complexion, reported to me about the farmhouse. I was situated underneath one of the abandoned squatters' huts on the outer limits of the village, doing my best to stay dry and make myself scarce with Mercer and Ashton, two of my most trusted infantrymen posted with me for security detail. He said there was a large hut down the hill, a half-click east of the village.

"I think there's a place for us to dig in, sir. It's a storage hut or something, about the size of one of the mobile mess halls. And it's filled with enough rice to feed a fuckin army. And it's got some kind of weird symbols and shit on it, sir," I remember him saying, and it got a laugh out of everyone, the way he said it, no one knowing just how literal he was being. In fact, that was one of the last things he told me. Although none of those men deserved to die, David Cuningham was a damn saint compared to some of those men. He never blew off steam in the miscreant ways some of the other privates did. He didn't reduce the enemy to numbers or mistreat the prisoners we took. He always wore his cross and prayed every morning before slops. He didn't get the privilege of dying quickly in his sleep like the others did a week later.

The hut was definitely some kind of grain storage facility, with enough rice to feed an actual platoon. This immediately sent up red flags in my mind, as all the huts we cleared appeared rather well-stocked for such an isolated mountain village, which told me they were supplying VC troops with food. Those damn symbols too... Christ. What appeared to be some kind of triangular mandala was painted all over the interior of the place in a dark, red fluid that dried to a hard crust. While I inspected the symbol, a few of the men, who appeared especially shaken, reported to me that they had seen that same sigil marked on all of the villagers they came across. About the size of a silver dollar and burned into the flesh at the nape of their necks. The villagers corroborated with the woman's story of a crazed rebel shaman who had placed this land under some kind of spell or curse. If this was a ploy or a distraction, then they sure as hell went the extra mile in theatrics.

As we began to move into the hut, setting out tarps and a few of the field tents for us to dry off in, a woman came running down the hillside, screaming and crying, running through the rain and slipping down the muddy slope. Mercer and Ashton immediately brought up the barrels of their M16s, tracking her.

"Sir?" Mercer asked, asking permission to neutralize.

"Stand down. She's nearly naked and her hands are empty. If she's got grenades, I don't see them," I said quickly, not wanting to escalate things.

The woman, who looked to be in her late forties, was suddenly right there, screaming at us, shoving us. She was naked from the waist down, her legs sporting bloody gashes that looked like claw marks, the ragged remnants of a robe or shawl hanging from her torso. I barked at Lu to come up and ask what she was yelling about. He tried to calm her down, but there was no reprieve from her state of abject terror. Lu listened, confusion and concern growing on his face. Finally, I stepped in and demanded a translation. Two men restrained the woman while I conversed with Lu.

"She says you have to leave now. Her son has already transformed and tried to kill her, and if we don't leave now, the rest of the village is going to turn and they will all—" but he was cut off as a commotion went on behind him. I walked past him and saw that the two men had let go of the woman. She had stopped yelling, and instead collapsed to the ground, her body contorting and twitching. She rolled around in the mud, grunting and convulsing. She voided her bowels as her body began to slowly change. I could hear her bones breaking and grinding over the dull roar of the rain. Her head elongated to strange dimensions, her arms growing longer, her fingers lengthening and sporting claws. We all watched silently, horrified, stunned at the site unfolding before us.

That was when she got on her hands and knees with catlike quickness and looked around with eyes that were pure white. Her mouth grew large and deformed, a long jaw that hung down, showing jagged, crooked teeth and a yellow tongue.

"Sir?" Mercer said again, his finger poised on the trigger of his rifle, a tremor in his voice. But before he could get off a shot, she lunged at Cuningham, who was standing the closest, watching with horror and fascination. She plunged her clawed hands into his stomach, and…I can still hear the sound of his guts slapping against the mud.

Mercer fired, but then his M16 jammed, because that's what M16s did exactly when you needed them the most. But his one stray shot broke our subdued awe, and in a split second, there came four quick bursts from four different guns, the goblin that was once a woman collapsing against Cuningham. She had been straddling the medic, her head buried in his throat when they unloaded on her. We pried her off him, and I saw that he was gone, Cuningham's throat a ragged gash and the purple and pink ropes of his plumbing splayed out in the mud, his eyes staring blankly up at the heavy wet clouds. I didn't even have time to mourn his death. We soon heard bestial ululations coming from the village above, the first wave of them charging down at us.

It all happened with chaotic speed, as if time had been sped up and the gates of hell had decided to open on that humble little piece of Vietnam. They came in droves, some running upright, others clambering on all fours in an animal-like locomotion, their deformed and clawed hands digging up clods of mud as they ran. All of them screamed in a high-pitched caterwauling that sounded like wolves howling through a concert PA system, like hell's own choir. Before I could give the order to open fire, my men, who had endured far more than any mortal man should have to, and who were only operating on sheer instinct, began lighting them up. The horde ran full charge, oblivious of the bullets that whistled past them. Their eyes shone like a cats' in the lights of the darting flashlights, their eyes nothing but white. Many had shed their clothes as their bodies transformed and their limbs rearranged into a corrupt anatomy, and I was afforded horribly vivid glances of those abominations as they jittered and twitched, holes opening up in their bodies as my men mowed them down without prejudice.

Someone—I think it may have been Mercer—tossed a couple frag grenades out. We had been bundled tightly into the hut, creating a solid firing line just like a formation out of the Civil War. Those in the front turned and shielded their faces from the blasts as organs, blood, and mud splashed back at us. A few of the monsters managed to take advantage in that momentary respite of rifle fire and break into the front line. I don't recall which of the men it was, but I saw two of them take their Ka-Bars out and begin grappling with the creatures, trying to get a blow in where they could. I heard a few screams from my men as teeth and claws met American flesh.

As I said, time seemed to warp as the creatures came down the hill, but I will hazard to estimate that a space of perhaps five minutes went by before the last ones were killed. Bodies littered the hillside, a torrent of rain-deluded blood washing down to us, the overwhelming smell of gore, human feces, and gun smoke hanging in the air. For a much longer time, we all stood there, huddled in the hut, rifles poised, eyes wide, muscles tense. I kept expecting enemy fire to start hurling down on us, but none came. Only the steady roar of rain swallowed up the cacophony of war. Eventually, I forced myself to be a captain again and decided we needed to check out the village, as they all appeared to originate from up there. Reluctantly, we moved out from our fire hole, walking through the sea of deformed corpses.

The village itself was totally empty, all the huts left in disarray as the villagers underwent their transformations—discarded bloody clothes and bed sheets lay everywhere. With that confirmed, I ordered my men to inhabit the nearest cluster of huts in the central part of the village, and to get some sleep. I know it may seem especially heinous that after we laid waste to those damned souls who attacked us, we slept in their beds and ate the remains of their food. But you were not there. I was simply doing what I had to do to ensure my men and I survived through the night and kept our sanity, although I doubt I succeeded in the latter.

It was in the morning, when the men, who all slept like the dead and woke to a silent and humid day, discovered the surprise waiting for us down the slope. One of the men doing a perimeter check had walked past the heap of bodies down the hill, which everyone else in the platoon made sure to avoid, and then reported back to me, his eyes wide and his demeanor nearly hysterical. Surely the man was cracking, going south, imagining things. But I went and saw for myself. He was right. What I saw was what you saw in the papers. Scores of dead South Vietnamese villagers of all ages and gender. Not monsters or demons or abominations, but regular human beings, their bodies destroyed by American weapons.

It was in that moment that I finally felt my resolve break. The voice in my mind that always told me to bite down and keep going, to see clearly in the heat of battle, shattered. And I have yet to regain it.

As I describe this scenario to you, I want to emphasize the fact that what I am relaying to you is God's honest truth. I have already admitted that some of my men fell victim to drug abuse, and many of them were probably not sober when this event occurred. But I was in my complete faculties at the time, despite being as stunned and sleep-deprived as I was. When it is my turn on the stand, when I face the judge and explain my role in what is being called the Qui Nang Massacre, I will tell them that what I saw was no mere hallucination, if I can even find the voice to speak. The notion that my men and I shared a group hallucination during those few hours we were stuck in that village is an outright, goddamned lie. Those abominations are forever seared into my memory. Those were not people we were firing at. At least not during that unknown stretch of time where we had to fend off those hordes of godless creations. I know I will be court-martialed and dishonorably discharged for this, probably thrown into a psychiatric hospital. And I will gladly go, but for those who expect my story to change or to assume that I am simply lying to cope with my own actions, you will be disappointed.

It should also be made explicitly clear that those were not *people* who slaughtered my men in their sleep. Cuningham may have been the only one to perish in battle, but several of my men sported severe cuts and lacerations, some of them becoming powerfully infected in the short time after the wounds were inflicted. The same day we made the horrible discovery, I radioed in to my superiors, explained the situation, omitting the details about anything supernatural, instead relaying that the entire village had turned hostile, and we had no choice but to open fire, which, is not exactly a lie, is it? Our job done, no real evidence of enemy matériel or ordinance in sight, we made the miserable trek back to the Mekong River insertion point, back to our firebase. The journey was just as long and miserable as before, even more so as we had to transport Cuningham's already bloated and rotting corpse with us back to the swift boat.

It was another S&D platoon that found the mound of bodies a few days later, the children, the women, the men, all shot indiscriminately like dogs, no sign of enemy weapons, just our spent shell casings. It was then that my superior officer called me into his office at Firebase Delta, informing me that an official investigation had just opened involving our brief occupation of Qui Nang. While my men walked around listlessly, staying mum on their experiences and some finding blissful oblivion in the sweet smoke of opium and cannabis, I broke down and told General Rogers exactly what happened. I even managed to sketch out the Mandala symbol I had seen on the side of the hut. I told him to interview my men, that they'd all say the same. That we lost our medic to those villagers, and that a few of the men had claw marks and other wounds to sport as evidence. Except that wasn't much evidence in itself, as it was common to come across surly panthers and other hostile fauna in the bush, in places where the war hadn't quite heated up, where the agent orange had yet to be dropped.

As you might expect, our story was met with great skepticism. My S.O.s reported directly to Westmoreland himself, and the last thing that man wanted to hear was of another FUBAR situation involving dead civilians. The attitude back home was turning cold really quickly, and apparently, our presence here was being mocked and ridiculed. The actions of my men had become a political nightmare for all high-ranking generals involved. I knew any minute some field journalist was going to catch wind of what happened, of a new controversy to stir the pot, and that's when I knew I was going to lose my job over this.

Three days after we returned from Qui Nang, my whole platoon was ordered to stay in the backup shelters behind the mess hall while they waited for more of the big brass to be flown in. A field investigation was to be done immediately. Those shelters, originally meant to house POWs temporarily, was in the least protected part of the firebase, but I have a feeling that what came in the night to steal those men's lives wouldn't have had a problem entering even if we were all huddled up in the general's quarters.

We were intentionally isolated, ordered not to fraternize with any of the other soldiers until the investigation was complete. We had been there for three days before the shadows came. I didn't sleep at all that night, but many of my men slept fitfully, some in a near-coma, somewhere close to death as they smoked themselves stupid, trying to forget about what they saw or to numb their terrible infected wounds. It was a depressing, cramped canvas prison, and as 0200 approached, and everyone was asleep, I noticed movement at the head of the shelter. A fluid, smooth movement, like smoke in the wind, flowing in from the cracks of the tarp door, consolidating itself into multiple small forms the size of children. These forms lined up at the foot of each cot, except mine. Like ethereal shadows that moved of their own volition, they floated over the beds, slowly sinking down, their small bodies inching toward the snoozing heads of my men as they tried to find reprieve from this living nightmare.

I thought perhaps I was hallucinating; the stress and trauma of the following days was surely enough to cause sleep-deprived delirium. I watched silently fascinated as the smoke-things disappeared into the men. That's when I began to hear the strangled coughs, the choking. All of them began to twitch and writhe, holding their throats, eyes bulging wide. Some managed to sit up, clawing out with their hands trying to find the source of whatever was cutting off their oxygen. Within a span of ten minutes, they were all dead, frozen in various poses of struggle. Once they all ceased moving, the smoke-things once again reappeared, and then reformed into one, looming figure that was nearly as tall as the tent ceiling. This figure stood above my own cot, as if deciding whether to spare me or not. For a very long time, it stood, watching me, studying me, before vaporizing into nothing.

THIS HAPPENED TWO WEEKS AGO. I have not found a reason as to why I was spared. Perhaps it was because I was not the one who did any of the firing. I didn't shoot a single bullet that day, but I still directed my men to become merchants of death. Perhaps I was left to survive because being forced to live the rest of my life, whatever may come of it, would be a worse punishment than killing me along with my men. Perhaps it was they who received the ultimate mercy. I don't know. All I know is that we are now facing an enemy that may have powers beyond what we can fathom. What other villagers out there in the isolated highlands face this same dilemma? Has some faction of the Vietcong managed to harness supernatural energies to help aid them in the war effort?

These are my concerns. Not that I will be locked away or have my reputation tarnished, but that a very real, unilateral threat to future soldiers lurks in that deep, unforgiving jungle. A threat that defies anything we've trained for. Those with access to the redacted files of Operation Paper Clip surely must know about the occult and supernatural goings-on we discovered among top Nazi scientists during our interrogations. Perhaps something similar, albeit primitive and crude, is being used deep in the high mountains of Qui Nang, and God knows where else. Already I have heard reports trickling in from other platoons that were forced to go out among the boundaries of the country, finding similar scenes and symbols among the villagers.

As a man of stern Christian faith and sound logic, what I have experienced has challenged my moral compass, my understanding of what is real and what is fantasy. As the days have gone by and I await my fate, I have slowly driven myself insane trying to make sense of it all. Two nights in a row, the smoke has returned, finding its way unhindered through the fortified walls of the firebase, looming over me, each time its shape becoming more real, consolidated.

It stands before me now as I write this, the form no longer ethereal smoke, but of a monstrous demon comprised of obsidian flesh and white eyes, a look of smug contempt on its inhuman face. I beg for it to kill me, to set my mind free of this constant internal turmoil. It is invisible to the other men who come in, responding to my cries of horror. They sedate me, threaten to restrain me, oblivious to the horror that occupies the room with them. Tonight, it has begun whispering to me, it's tongue Vietnamese. While my knowledge of the language is rudimentary at best, the phrase it repeats over and over in my waking nightmares is clearly understood:

Your soul is mine to haunt.

8

SONS OF LUNA

THE TIRES of Bruce Mayton's old Chevy crunched and crackled over the gravel as he pulled into the bar's parking lot. It was empty, save for the four other vehicles he knew would be here. He got out, swatting at the tide of mosquitos swirling in the air. Before going in, he turned to look at the lake across the road from the bar. The moon was full and commanding, it's radiant-luminescence washing the whole area in a hazy glow and shimmering off the mirror of lake water. In the distance he could see the cypress trees stationed from the bank extending out into the lake, like silent guardsmen between the normal world, and the world he was about to enter.

He had a feeling, not a good one, but a feeling. He sighed, and walked up to The Crow's Nest main entrance, *The Open-Cold Beer Awaits* sign was off. He pulled open the dented screen–door and knocked on the metal door within. Four sharp hits, their simple code. A moment went by, and then he heard the deadbolt sliding before the door opened.

He was looking at the face of Susan Carter, John's daughter. She was in a tank top with the bar logo on it, a crow with an eye patch, which she designed herself, and blue jeans, her red hair pulled back in a sweaty bun. Her face was haggard.

"You're late. Get in here."

"Gangs all here," John said, as he walked up to shake Bruce's hand.

The two hard, callused hands clasped in a vice grip. He did the same with David and Buck, who were in the middle of a game of eight ball when he walked in.

"Can I get you somethin'?" Susan asked from behind the bar. She was cleaning glasses and trying to make herself scarce.

"Sure thing, hon. A whiskey and coke on the rocks," said Bruce.

She nodded and poured the Jim Beam into a tumbler, her hands trembling, causing her to spill some.

"Shit," she said, under her breath. She put the drink on the counter.

Bruce took it, and then put his large hand on hers before she could get a chance to move away and clean up the mess.

"You alright?" he asked quietly. It was a stupid question, but he felt the need to ask it. Susan was like a daughter to him, and he hated seeing her this tense, like some invisible gun was pointed at her.

"What do you think, Bruce? Every goddamn year I gotta watch y'all play this game of Russian roulette, and every year I gotta wonder if it's gonna be my dad this time."

"It won't be this year, I promise," he said, after a moment.

"You don't know that. You know you don't. Now go over there and get it done already!" She jerked her hand away.

Bruce took a deep drink as he walked over to the center of the small bar. All the stools and chairs were put up on the nearby tables, except one. A round, wooden table was set out in the middle, and sitting on top of it was a jar filled with water. It was hard to see in the dim glow of the bar lights, but Bruce knew it was going to be dingy, bits of algae and bacteria floating around in the lake water.

Every year since his 6th birthday he had been forced to participate in the ritual, which was thirty years to this day, back when this communion was much larger, and he had never once been sick from drinking the water. He just knew, tonight was the night. He felt it in his old bones. He had a dream, a dream that *he* was the chosen one. That *he* would be the next harbinger. He kissed his wife extra hard, and gave his son a long hug, trying to cherish their scents, their feelings, their faces before he headed out to the Crow's Nest.

"We gotta hurry, the moon's already starting to turn," said Buck, as he looked out one filmy window at the reddening globe.

Susan gave her father four solo cups, and he distributed these out to the other men, leaving one for himself. For a moment they all just stood there, none of them wanting to be the one who touched the jar.

"I just collected it this morning. Get on with it now," Susan said impatiently.

"Yeah yeah," Bruce said.

With a hand that betrayed only the slightest tremble, he reached out and grabbed the mason jar, pouring a shot into the bottom of his cup. He then poured for each of the men around the table until the jar was empty. They all looked into their cups for a moment, and then Bruce raised his up.

"Cheers, fellas," he said sarcastically, and knocked back the warm lake water.

He had to stifle a gag as he choked it down, the taste of dirt and algae coalescing with the burn of cheap whiskey in his throat. There were likewise gurgles and gags around as all four men ingested Lake Myerla.

Bruce then slammed back the rest of his whiskey and coke. For a moment, he had to stick his tongue to the roof of his mouth and squeeze his eyes shut. For thirty years he'd been choking the shit down, and it never got any easier.

"Alright, we got twenty minutes. Let's get out on the water before one of us makes a mess in here," John said, walking out the door.

The men silently exited behind him, all of them outwardly stoic, but inwardly terrified.

Buck's boat was already in the water, sidled up to the dock. They made their way clumsily into the old john boat and helped shove off. Buck had to pilot the boat carefully around the many cypress roots until they were further out, the trees eventually thinning out into a circle out in the middle of the lake, where the island was. The island where they were all born, on the same day, September 23rd, 1970. It was known reverently in their small community as "the year of the reckoning."

They kept their heads low as they passed over the thick webs of the Saint Andrew's cross spiders, their gossamer homes made messy with dead cicadas, moths and mosquitos. The large spiders, some as big as dinner plates, fidgeted and moved around their interconnected webs as the men passed by below.

It was a 400 acre circular lake, with the island, known locally as "Fortress of the Flock," located directly in the center. The surrounding counties treated the place like a leper colony, despite The Flock being quiet, respectful folk who only came off the island to get farming supplies. They dressed the same and held similar beliefs to the Mennonites of the region, yet they did not worship Jesus Christ. It wasn't until a defector left the island that rumors of pagan rituals and worship, as well as child sacrifice, had spread far and wide, until the small sect caught the attention of state child welfare services.

Despite the run-down shacks with broken windows, overgrown weeds, and the derelict aluminum shed used as a town hall, they still remembered their bustling childhood home as the idealistic utopia it had been. Each one had their own bittersweet memories of what they thought of as home, at least until the government had intervened.

All of the children had gone through intensive "debriefing" therapies in an attempt to integrate them back into the society they had been so fervently protected from. They'd all made good progress, recognizing many of the forced behaviors and superstitions they'd grown up to obey were, in fact, abuse, and the consequences fictional. However, the therapists couldn't change their belief regarding the "Ushering of the Equinox" ceremonies.

From the Flock's inception in 1965 to their collapse in 1980, there were over one hundred children born on the island, but it was the cluster of children who were born in 1970 that would change the ways of the commune forever. Bruce and the other three surviving members were part of the group of 32 males who were born on September 23rd, 1970, a statistical anomaly, in terms of gender probability. All 100 children had reported seeing the same disturbing and fantastical scenes every year on that day afterwards. After several failed attempts to get the children to realize that what they saw wasn't real, the state psychologists acquiesced and ruled it a group hallucination.

Here they were, over 30 years later, the last survivors of an extremist religious sect that worshipped the moon and believed that continuous sacrifice to the lunar gods was the only way to spare the earth from imminent apocalypse. Psychologists called it *catastrophizing*. This was a common symptom of people suffering from obsessive-compulsive disorder: A firm belief that failure to complete whatever mundane ritual they believed necessary to live would result in devastating consequences.

These same psychologists glossed over the fact that, from 1980-1983, when the surviving members of The Flock were not allowed to travel back to the island for those three years, three members of their group had all died horribly in random, freak accidents. Also unaccounted for was that, during those three years, the planet had experienced a slew of natural disasters that had culled over 200,000 people. Freak earthquakes that happened in heavily populated areas where no active fault lines were known to exist. Abnormally large and powerful hurricanes that hit off season in places where mild tropical depressions only existed. Two volcanoes that erupted simultaneously, one in Hawaii and one in Brazil, another statistical anomaly that was unexplained.

And Bruce was sure the group of well-meaning researchers and psychologists would be sorely disappointed if they learned that these now grown men had begun to meet in secret at their old home again every year, and participate in the Ushering of the Equinox ritual yet again. He was sure words like *shared hallucinations, recidivism,* and *unresolved trauma* would be applied to their situation, which was fine with him, because those psychologists and therapists, while well intentioned, didn't know a goddamned thing.

They had reached the muddy bank of the island, and all four of them got out, helping to beach the boat. Bruce walked along the shore, staring at the moon as it rippled on the water, wavering and dancing in the chop caused by the boat. They had all been birthed in this lake, baptized in its waters. He could remember their teachings clearly, the myths and mysticism that shrouded this place.

This body of water being chosen and christened by the founding members of the Flock, all of whom were female, as the place where the ground was thin, where it was easiest for the beings who operated in sync with the cycles of the moon to break through and accept the offerings bestowed upon them by the Flock. The offerings always had to be male. The particular lunar being they prayed to was a goddess, and according to the Flock's beliefs, this goddess demanded the chaotic, aggressive energy of the male in order to restore balance to the Mother, the Earth itself.

They saw Earth as an autonomous living being, the active caretaker of all life living upon its flesh. They saw the Moon as the sister, the helping hand in keeping the Earth's natural processes balanced. Bruce and the other 31 males born in the lake that year served as the offerings to restore this balance, their sacrificed blood and souls serving as the currency that bought the world another year of peace and harmonious existence, as had the previous generations before them, according to the Elders.

"How's everyone feeling?" asked Buck as he walked, examining the island as he walked along the bank.

The men all grumbled vaguely.

Each of them knew it would happen suddenly, all of them flinching at the slightest movements or noise, all of them on edge. When there was greater numbers of the 1970 group, things weren't as tense, as the diffusion of responsibility was greater. 1 in 30 wasn't as bad as 1 in 4. It was easier to think *no, it couldn't be me, it's gonna be him, or him, or him*. But with every year that they reconvened, and every time the group grew smaller, it was harder to think that way. Last year was real bad. That was when Joseph Mattis was taken. That one stuck with Bruce.

Joseph had been one of Bruce's best friends, one of the few people from the group with whom he'd formed a true bond. Although all of the males had moved close to Myerla Lake and kept in touch out of formal necessity, Joseph and Bruce had a genuine bond. Their kids had played together, their wives ate brunch together. They had family cookouts. Joseph and Bruce shared the deep connection of experiencing things that no one else had lived through. They were like veterans who had survived a horrible war, and could only confide in each other about the traumas and private agonies they had endured.

It was simply easier when there were more of them.

They all walked around anxiously, inspecting the ruins of the buildings, looking at each other with passing glances, seeing who would double over. The waiting, that was worst part for all of them... Well, until it became clear who the chosen one was. For whoever that was, their last moments would be unfathomable agony.

Then, all at once, they looked up at the moon, which already took up a large portion of the sky as it grew towards the apex of its cycle. Each one felt the invisible, familiar pull. They were hypnotized by the great God in the sky, this moment, this magnetism towards the moon always serving as the prelude to Her arrival. The moon had grown into a huge, red leviathan until it was their entire world, their eyes dilated wide. They felt the sensation of falling up, into the crimson sphere, and that's when they knew she was almost here.

Anxiety and exhilaration filled Bruce and the other members as they experienced that familiar sensation that marked her passage into this dimension. The dilation of time, an adrenaline fueled slowing of their perceptions, which preceded her arrival.

Finally, with a resounding *boom*, like a jet breaking the sound barrier, the spell was broken, and the long, drawn-out moment of climax was finally here.

THE SOUND of vomit splattering on the ground was the first sound Bruce heard after his ears recovered from the blast. The sensation of serene weightlessness from the lunar-induced trance abruptly ceased, and Bruce felt himself slam back into his body. His whole body immediately tensed as he knew this meant the hunt was on. He tore his gaze away from the moon, his vision stained with it's vivid after-image and through the negative blob of color he could sense movement. He heard moans coming to his right, and tried to remember who had walked over there.

I wasn't chosen, it was the only thing he could think as his senses slowly returned to normal.

Bruce could faintly hear a voice partially muffled by a low thrumming, like a powerful electric current.

"Please…No. My daughter. Please!"

Her frequency was the frequency of life, of tidal power, of being. She was somewhere close by, and Bruce instinctively backed away, towards the water. He knew no harm would come to him now, but still, his animal instincts screamed for him to run.

As his vision cleared, the dark surroundings of the island began to take shape. He saw John on his knees, twenty feet away, his eyes were bulging as he wept blood. Bruce saw that his nose, ears and mouth also trickled blood, and in front of the man was a large pile of vomit. John was trying to turn away, but couldn't. His body trembled as he tried to break free from her hold, but it was useless.

John's gaze was directed right behind Bruce's shoulder. Unable to help himself, Bruce turned, and followed his gaze. There was the slight distortion of the night sky as something partially invisible moved, then slowly materialized into a twenty foot, humanoid-shaped silhouette. The edges of the silhouette distorted the air around it, like an all-consuming black hole.

She passed Bruce in a slow, elegant walk that defined her edges more clearly with every step, until she was the gray, radiant being that had appeared in their nightmares. Her feminine curves became more pronounced, which contrasted with the hunched over, almost crude posture she took as she bent down to examine John. She appeared to be made of the water itself, a shimmering luminescent figure with two pure white eyes in her head, and glowing pond moss for hair.

Submit.

Bruce heard the word in his gut.

Submit.

Though directed at John, all four men sank to their knees, silently weeping, their eyes staring at her form.

"No!" John screamed. "I won't! I wo—"

Submit, she repeated.

Blood began to bead and trickle from John's flesh like crimson sweat.

"N-No!" He repeated, his voice strained with the wet, ripping sound of rupturing vocal chords.

Submit.

The voice like a thousand whispers, like the sound of all the insects in the world, like the splintering of every tree on the planet, slammed into their heads.

Bruce felt a spike of pain lance his skull at the final commandment, and felt a warmth trickling from his nose.

With this last repetition, John let out a final scream, which sounded more like a ragged squeal, and then he simply exploded. The sound of viscera and organs splattering upon the ground was swiftly accompanied by the coppery smell of gore.

Just like that, she was gone. Bruce looked around dazed, still reeling from the sudden violence of it all. In the pale light of the moon, he could see the puddles and lumps of flesh strewn about him. He saw these puddles begin to bubble up, and slowly disappear, the bones liquefying. John Carter's body was being reabsorbed by the planet he was cursed to protect. Balance was restored, once again.

It wasn't me...

As soon as Susan heard the boom, she knew that one of them was about to die. Her father had gone to great lengths to try and explain his situation to her as a kid. How daddy had a different upbringing from other folks, how he had a special commitment to his extended family, his *other* family. For a while, she'd suspected her father and all his friends were completely insane as each year they met up at some small lake she'd never heard of, with one of them never coming back, never being heard from again. Then John had decided to open up the bar, and when she was old enough, hired Susan as a bartender. Eventually she was exposed to their ritual, which was always antecedent to the funerals she and her father attended. Year by year, she had to reconcile that either she was going insane, or that her father was actually cursed by some long defunct cult.

It was his idea to open the bar at the lake's edge and keep some kind of connections around the land so that way they would have a place to recover when the ritual concluded. This was her fifth year working at the Crow's Nest, begrudgingly learning the family business and postponing her hopes of travelling west to go to art school.

It was quiet out here for the most part, with the lowly fisherman or hunter from around the county coming in to drink quietly. But she hated the summer, and the months filled with heat, bugs and tourists leading to September. Those five years of service at the Crow's Nest saw her tending to first ten men, and then nine, until only the four were left. They always came back haunted, quiet and shaken, sometimes covered in blood. Some borderline catatonic with shock. How they managed to do this every year without losing their minds was beyond her. In some ways, she wished her father had kept his goddamned secret. She had been living year to year in a perpetual state of tension, bracing herself for the tragedy that never came.

She was sitting in a corner of the bar, nursing a beer with a shaking hand, counting the minutes since she heard the explosion. A half hour later, she heard the screen door open, and she silently regarded the three haggard looking men who stood before her. She noted the absence in the group, nodded silently, and then only sat there. Tears began to crawl down her face. She took another pull from the beer, half choking as a sob exploded out of her.

"Susan- " Bruce began.

"Don't. Just fucking...don't. Get out of here. All of you. I'm done. I'm done with this stupid fucking game, this stupid ritual, this whole goddamn place!" She threw the beer bottle behind the bar.

Glass shattered, and the aroma of cheap whiskey filled the air. She took the zippo from her jeans pocket, a birthday gift from her father, flicked it open, and tossed it into the growing puddle of whiskey and glass, igniting it with a *whoomph*. The flames quickly spread up the old wooden cabinets of the bar, alighting a box of cardboard coasters, which only served to fuel the fire even more.

She walked past the men and out the door.

"Jesus, Susan!" Buck yelled, searching around for something to douse the flames with. He ran past David and Bruce, directing them to get water from the lake.

David ran after him, and Bruce slowly followed. When the two men came back with bucketfuls of lake water, Bruce grabbed both their arms.

"Let it burn, yall. Just...let it burn," he said calmly.

The two men looked at Bruce incredulously, then at the bar, and dropped their buckets and took a step back.

The flames were spreading quickly, and smoke was already billowing out from the screen door. The bar was so far out from any service road or county highway that it would be too late before emergency services arrived, the structure would surely be consumed by fire.

Bruce regarded the men before him. He didn't know either one particularly well. John was the second closest friend he'd had in the group. Buck and David were two farmers who lived up north, both trying to forget about their fates as much as possible, both keeping minimum contact with their fellow sons of Luna. Both telling their families that it was a yearly hunting trip they always went on, not a gathering, not an Ushering of the Equinox.

Bruce hoped it would be him next year. He was tired of doing this. He was tired of waiting. His family was dysfunctional at best, his wife often having frequent panic attacks from the constant reminder of her husband's eventual fate. He was exhausted. Every year that he had to endure another sacrifice, he felt a piece of himself go back with Her. Like Susan, the toll of living with constant uncertainty had driven him down into the abyssal depths of alcoholism. He suspected the others who were left, his fellow sons of Luna, had similar coping vices.

"What's gonna happen when the last one of us is taken?" David wondered aloud. "They didn't tell us about that. What happens after?"

Bruce shrugged, and regarded the moon again. Such a seemingly benign entity, but with the power to decide the fate of all humanity. Bruce often wondered what would become of this place once the ritual finally concluded. His parents had told him that the cycle always repeats, that the Mother and the Sister always found a way to achieve balance.

"I don't know," Bruce said finally, "but at least it won't be our problem anymore."

9

THE CHIWAA'E

Most people who know me these days would never believe I was a long haul truck driver. Being a reclusive leathery old man who refuses to drive any sort of automobile and attends AA meetings every Sunday, it's understandable where the incredulity would come from. The only people who know of my true past are the few remaining family members I have, and of them, the only one who still speaks to me (at least acknowledges my presence as a human being) is Johnathan, my cousin, who ironically enough is the one who got me the job with Davison International.

I sense Johnathan has always been more understanding of my situation because he holds more to the traditional values of *our people* than everyone else in the family. I am only 40% Navajo by blood, the rest, to the blight of my ancestors, is a mix of European lineage, my parents being the mixed offspring of white roughnecks in oil boom towns who invaded the local bars and eateries where many on the reservations worked to make some pittance of income. Johnathan, like his parents, whose father was the brother of my own father, happened to stay on the reservation when so many of us left, going for greener pastures in the suburbs and the cities. He became one of those rare traditionalists, who tried to keep the spirit of our ancestors alive when apathy and vice claimed most of the rest of us.

Davison International was one of those progressive companies that prided itself on its diversity and racial quota. Part of their mission statement was hiring people from "disadvantaged backgrounds" and helping those who needed to turn a new leaf, so when I came looking to apply on my cousin's recommendation, with a DUI and reckless manslaughter charge on my file, George Howell, who would eventually go on to be my boss, gave me a chance. He took me into a back office, where he reviewed my otherwise stellar driving record as a mid-range driver for DHL and Wabash, the latter I happened to be driving for when the accident happened. An accident resulting in a gross loss of life, but I was so piss drunk and blacked out I don't remember it.

"I expect two things of you, Robert," he said, "Is that your actual name or just the name the white man gave you?" He said with a laugh. I didn't really know what he meant by that, but he continued on before I could clarify, "Anyway, what I expect of you is to be straight with me. I need drivers I can trust, who are reliable. I need drivers who can work these eighteen-hour routes and meet deadlines without getting hooked on ice or speed in the process. You get my product where it needs to be and my truck back here on time, I will pay you better than any son of a bitch will, given your circumstances. Can you do that for me?"

I did it for him, to the best of my ability.

JOHNATHAN WAS the one who told me to apply for the long-haul trips. They were tough, fourteen to eighteen hour stretches on occasionally hazardous roadways. It was he who informed me that some of the biggest paying hauls were those done by companies in the out-of-the-way oil boom towns which were now so much reclaimed desert and desolation, the roads leading to them perilous, ensuring generous hazard pay. The longest drive I had ever done before applying there was an eight hour trip to go see my Nana on my mother's side out in Nevada. But George was an intuitive man, and something in his gut told him I was the man for the job. Perhaps the fact I still had to do monthly urinalysis screenings with my probation officer also told him I was on a short leash and not likely to be giving into the usual highway vices.

Indeed, after the accident I was a soul set on salvation. I was a man of God for a short while, as the folks at AA usually nudge towards relying on a higher power to help deal with the guilt and stress of addiction. I was incredibly thankful for my job at DI trucking, and was dead set on not disappointing the two people who'd given me the chance. I threw myself at the job, taking the longer, harder routes that most veterans wouldn't even take. A seventeen-hour drive to Cut Bank, Montana, delivering imported hardwoods to a specialty craftsman shop tucked away in the mountains was my trial by fire, with the journey entailing me driving along US81, one of the more winding, treacherous routes through the Rockies, which just so happened to be blanketed with snow during my trip.

This was then followed by a nerve wracking eighteen-hour drive to Fareway, North Dakota, right next to the Canadian border and the only road going in and out of it being a narrow two-lane state highway that went up several steep changing grades and a few bridges that looked like they hadn't seen roadwork since FDR was president. I completed several more drives like this, without ever being pulled over for skipping weigh-ins, while always pissing clean and having an exemplary delivery time. By the time I had been selected to make the drive out to Carroway's Peak, Arizona, I was rather infamous at Davison for being the dare devil among the roster of drivers. As progressed as a driver, George used me as a proud PR piece for a lot of his hiring campaigns and commercials, and Johnathan boasted of my seemingly noble fresh start in life to those distant relatives who still considered me a stain on the family mantel.

Which is why I was so taken aback when Johnathan, of all people, tried to talk me out of making the Arizona delivery. I worked at the Kansas City branch of Davison's distribution center, and the drive was roughly sixteen hours to Carroway's Peak, according to my GPS. I had never made deliveries to Arizona specifically before, but I had driven large portions of I-85 before going through Oklahoma and Texas, and it was easy country, a cakewalk compared to some of the other routes I'd been on. When I asked where his apprehension came from, he told me I would think he was dumb or getting all old-world spiritual, if he tried to explain. When he saw I was going to take the route regardless of his pleading, he pulled me aside while the semi was being loaded up.

"I know you're confused by my objections. Let me tell you though, it is not the road you have to worry about. Carroway's Peak is in a very... bad part of the Navajo Nation. It is on the Brownstone reserve, one of the most isolated reservations in all of the nations. I have heard many bad stories from people who have driven through there. It is not a good place for people like you. People whose hearts are vulnerable to the void. All the land around there... it is tainted. Bad energy roams that place. Please, for the sake of your sanity and your safety, make haste on your journey if you will not reconsider. Pay close attention to your surroundings, do not let yourself get distracted. There are entities that roam the thin veil between these worlds, Robert, and in places like Brownstone, that veil is practically non-existent."

THE ENDLESS BLACKTOP stretched out in front of me, the truck's cabin vibrating beneath my feet as I hurled my hulk of oil and steel through space, my cousin's ominous words still ringing in my ears. Part of me thought he was playing some kind of weird prank on me, while another part thought he wanted to instill those old-world superstitions into me as a cautionary tale not to drink. The latter, he wouldn't have to worry about, because even though I did have cravings, the occasional yearning for oblivion, the very thought of what that drink might lead to stopped me cold. Those revelations of killing people while in my stupor, the trial, the hellish withdrawals, the seven years I wasted away in jail, were all enough to bring me near the point of a full-blown panic attack anytime I contemplated wetting my whistle.

So, I decided not to think about his words, and I drove. I found that completely occupying myself with the task at hand was the best way to fight the malingering thoughts and anxiety that drove me to my cravings. Keep an eye on the RPM gauge, always keep a look out for the weigh stations. Watch your mirrors. Remember to log your hours. Remember when to shift, don't grind the gears. I had an old Sony boombox I kept tucked by the CB, and when the shakes came upon me or I felt myself slipping into an anxiety attack, I would put on Johnny Cash or Dwight Yokum or some other southern crooner that I knew so well and force myself to sing along, open up my airways and let the calming oxygen permeate my blood. I turned on the boombox and began to sing about Folsom Prison in my best Cash bravado.

I took I-35 down through the rolling corn fields of Kansas, passing through monotonous greenery before hitting Wichita and heading west. I passed through the narrow nose of Oklahoma and its smatters of suburbia and woods, taking US-54 briefly through Texas, seeing my first shades of what was to become a very long stretch of brown as I began to enter desert country. Then I was in the truly dry state of New Mexico, seeing jagged brown peaks in the distance and nothing but eroded barren topsoil, before dusk came and my world was reduced to headlights and taillights, pavement markings and the ever present OPEN/CLOSE of the ubiquitous interstate chicken coops I was required to stop at. Somewhere along the way I pulled into a Love's truck stop to fill up, the chill of the desert night biting into me as I went to stretch my legs and grab a coffee along with whatever greasy hand-held food they had rotating in the heat lamps.

At that point it had been just like any other trip I would've taken. As I hopped back into the cab and double checked my GPS, I noted that I would get to Carroway's Peak somewhere around four in the morning, which was exactly when the specialty warehouse there would be expecting me. Somewhere in the back of my mind I noted that in about six hours, I would be within the jurisdiction of

Johnathan's so called *bad lands*. Upon thinking of him, I pulled my cellphone from the center console and turned it on, checking to see if I had any route updates I needed to know about.

Hey, please let me know when you're on the way back. This isn't a request from DI. Just humor your old school peyote eating cousin -J

As I passed through Albuquerque in a blur of concrete and glass, I sung from the top of my lungs about a Mississippi woman and a Louisiana Man, gettin' together every time they can, forcing myself to belt out the oily snakes of dread that cinched around my stomach, causing the over-cooked burrito I ate to roil in my guts like something alive and malevolent. Soon I found myself yearning for city lights as unending shades of gray pressed upon me on both sides while I piloted a forty-ton missile into the heart of the desert. The night sky was vast and vivid with stars, the cosmos increasing with its luminous brilliance the further from civilization I drove.

At some point along my journey through I-40, my GPS told me to turn off onto US-51, which turned out to be one of the longest, loneliest stretches of two lane road I'd ever taken. That dusty old sign has been the screen opener of all my nightmares since. I drove, truly in the blasted desert land now, winding blacktop taking me through a monochromatic gray abyss until I saw a sign that said ENTERING HOPI NATION, TRIBAL POLICE JURISDICTION.

I was never as studious about my roots as Johnathan was; I didn't really know what my relation was to the Hopi people. But the land looked just the same as the last hundred or so miles I'd travelled, save for a few small townships that looked run down, defeated by time and circumstance. Eventually I came across a sign that read STOP NOW, NO GAS/ UTILITIES/ RESTAURANTS NEXT 150 MI and I raised my eyebrows at this.

The gas gauge was hovering just above the halfway point, which I mentally calculated as 200 miles if the going was easy. The thought of being stranded out there in that dry abyss caused various orifices in my body to tighten, so I pulled into one of the most depressing looking, scabrous truck stops I had ever seen, using a pump that still had rotating panel numbers instead of a digital screen. Inside I grabbed some coffee and the cashier, a man who could've been my grandfather, told me the total, then added something in Navajo at the end.

When he saw I didn't understand what he was saying, he scowled with disgust and shooed me out the door, calling me something I'm sure translated into something like *uncultured mudblood asshole* in his native tongue. As I climbed back into the truck, sipping my watery coffee, I tried to look out into the desert night. But now the sky was overcast, a solid slate gray ceiling above me, the light from the stars suffocated, causing the horizon to look like the road simply trailed off towards the edge of the earth some two hundred feet beyond the arc sodiums of the gas station.

I felt a distinctly unwelcome presence here, as if everyone on the whole reservation knew who I was and what I did. The silence disturbed me as well, as I was used to the accustomed chorus of cicadas and crickets from my midwestern roots, but here it was just the rocks and sand, and absolutely nothing else, no sound at all. The land around me seemed to be holding its breath, ready to implode at any moment. I started the truck and reluctantly pulled out onto US-51, feeling like I was about to ride a tar-ridden vein into the atrium of some diseased heart.

IT WAS right after I reached mile marker 87 that I began to see the thing out of the corner of my eye. I was trying to sing about how all my exes lived in Texas, keeping myself awake and alert as I travelled a road that was completely straight and unchanging, my head lights only illuminating some ten feet on either side of me. I saw the occasional cactus and bloated armadillo, things that reminded me I was still on earth and not travelling some vast purgatory towards oblivion. No matter how much I tried to sing however, the tension filled my body, every muscle feeling like a bridge cable about to snap. This feeling only intensified when I first saw it.

At first I thought it was a coyote, which was a common enough sight in the desert. It darted out in front of the truck once in a black blur of movement. This struck me as odd. It was not the dull brown of a coyote, at least from what I could see, but left an ebony blur, like a black dog. I tried to tell myself it was possible that there was a pack of feral dogs out here. I drove for another five miles, trying to forget about it, when it happened again. It moved so quick I could not make out the details other than its approximate color. This time I swerved just a little, the trailer wobbling slightly as I corrected the course I was on.

"What the fuck," I said as I blinked, trying to clear my vision. *It's not a good place for people like you.* Johnathan's words came to me over the shuffle of steel guitar and waltzing drums as Hank Williams filled what now felt like a sealed pressure chamber. Then I saw the sign. A huge chunk of rock the size of my trailer, the words engraved and then painted into the beveled boulder raced up from the night to meet me, its presence distracting me momentarily. *NOW ENTERING BROWNSTONE RESERVATION.* I thought to myself that couldn't be right, as I had been keeping track of my miles since departing from that barren truck stop. I was only eighty miles in, which meant that Brownstone was much larger than I thought.

It doesn't matter how big it is, there's nothing out here that can—

It happened again, this time the creature appeared even closer, it's head in profile to the headlights. I saw a bright flash of light-reflecting eyes, intense enough to burn an after image of two blotchy orbs into my retinas. I swerved again, desperately trying to blink away the blobs obscuring my vision. I didn't know which idea was more terrifying, that this was one creature who was somehow able to keep up with my seventy mile an hour big rig, or that a pack of these goddamn things was playing chicken with my truck. I soon found the answer to my question as my vision returned. I tried to focus on the road, but I couldn't help but notice the blur of movement to the left of my peripheral vision.

It remained steady, unwavering, a galloping motion to it. *No, not possible. You're just seeing shit man. Should have slept more before you left.* I saw with some immense sense of relief that a small tinkling star of headlights could be seen some distance away. The fact I saw someone else out here, something to banish the overwhelming sense of isolation and utter wrongness made me ease up slightly on the steering wheel, which I'd been literally white-knuckling since leaving the truck stop. I slipped up then, letting my guard down and decided to turn my head, daring to confront the creature that was taunting me, following alongside my truck effortlessly.

At first, I couldn't understand what I was looking at. It ran like a canine, but its feet did not seem to touch the ground. It appeared to be made of a shadow, as it cast a black trail behind it like a jet leaving contrails. Before I could take in the rest of its anatomy however, its eyes found me, radiating like hateful coals in a wicked fire. When our eyes came together, I began to feel a profound disconnect from my body. It was close to the feeling one gets when imbibing in potent cannabis after reaching maximum intoxication with alcohol, a feeling of the room you were in spinning on an axis independent of your own.

I remember hearing myself say "Oh fuck" from outside the truck as the cab and the world around me evaporated.

THE FLASH OF HEADLIGHTS, the honking of a horn, the screech of tires. These things assault me simultaneously as I am abruptly slammed back into my body. But my surroundings are different. I'm no longer in the Kenworth eighteen-wheeler. I'm in the much smaller confines of my old DHL delivery van, which was still a large, heavy vehicle compared to the Cadillac I was milliseconds from side-swiping. I just have time to register the speedometer hovering at ninety when my world explodes with a scream of tearing metal and glass spiderwebs, which soon burst and tear my face open. I'm thrown forward by the hand of God, who must have surely meant for me to die here, to terminate my own useless soul and not the four-year-old girl and the forty-eight-year-old man who'd been driving his wife and daughter home from a dance recital on this terrible night.

I watch in excruciating slow motion as the car does a barrel roll in front of me, my front end crumpled and slowly lifting into the air from the impact. A small head with long dark hair smashes off the door window, the body briefly suspended in air as the sedan's metal framework implodes, swallowing her. Once, twice, three times the car rolls, all the while my van is right on its heels as inertia carries us both forward. Then this hellish vision speeds up, and I'm jostled and thrown around in my seat as the van collides yet again with the Cadillac before finally, my extremely delayed reaction to turn the tires hard to the right catches up with the rest of the world. The van fishtails, and I feel myself falling to the left as the van flops on its side.

Despite my belligerent inebriation before stepping behind the wheel, I'd somehow had the presence of mind to buckle my seatbelt prior to taking off for my route. Shaken, dazed, and without the numbing buffer of alcohol to spare me the horror of my actions, I unbuckle the seatbelt as it cuts into my waist, and I fall across the seat and slump against the door. Eventually, I'm able to climb out and fall to the pavement, where I land in a puddle of transmission fluid and gas. I begin to crawl on my hands and knees, trying to get away from the noxious odors of the car's spilled fluids, and manage to make my way over to the Cadillac, which is almost unrecognizable in its smashed and brutalized state.

It was an inner-city road we were on, with halogen lamps every forty feet. It was under one of these numerous domes of light where the car comes to a stop. I see a dark fluid draining from the corner of one of the crumpled doors. I see several large splashes of red against the car's deformed interior. A head lolls at an unnatural angle from a neck that has a chunk of sheered metal protruding from it. Blood spurts from the wound. I walk around to the other side of the car and gasp, seeing the mangled half of a small body laid out on the road. It was then I feel my gorge rise, knowing I'm about vomit up the gallon of Kentucky Gentleman I drank hours ago. I bend over, ready to purge the bloating acidic tide in my stomach as I start to hear screaming.

As if waking up from a dream within a dream, I came back inside the elevated cab of the Kenworth, and a jet of half-digested burrito and shitty coffee spewed out of my mouth, splashing the steering wheel before I can comprehend what is happening. The truck swerved as I lost control for a second, the headlights of the approaching vehicle much closer now than they were before. I didn't have time to contemplate how long I was in that alternate world, nightmare, whatever you want to call it, because I saw the creature was still running alongside the truck, trying to get out in front of me, I could see its eyes blazing as it turned to look at me, daring me to meet its gaze once again. I slammed one foot on the accelerator, shifting up, understanding that if this thing got out in front of me I would surely die.

I saw that the vehicle approaching me was also a semi, its huge white cab materializing behind the headlights like a dragon's head. His horn blared as he too saw the specter racing alongside me. *He sees it too, holy shit he sees*-I began to think, but it happened before I could finish the thought. The thing jumped up, I thought it was trying to make a last minute break for my grill before the oncoming truck obliterates it. Instead, it jumped head long into the snarling engine and hood of the other truck. For a few seconds my windshield was obscured in a black cloud as the wind and horn blasted from the other semi buffets my truck.

In a flash, it was gone, the cloud dissipating, the taillights of the other truck in my rearview. By sheer force of will I kept the truck straight despite my whole body trembling. The road did not change at all for the next sixty miles, and I drove it in a blur, vomit drying on the dashboard, my GPS warning me that I was exceeding the posted speed limit and not caring. Knowing this violation would be logged on the truck's onboard computer that fed data back to the warehouse analysts, resulting in points docked and a warning, made no difference to me; I needed to be off this goddamn road.

I thought I would see welcoming civilization when I approached Carroway's Peak. Instead I found a depressing little township with one stoplight and a smattering of shotgun shacks and run down trailers, with a small thoroughfare that held an all-night diner, a small gas station, and the white brick building with faded lettering which said JOE'S FOOD CO-OP, whose canned and dry goods I had driven all this way to deliver. I realized with some embarrassment that I did not bring a change of clothes with me, and the front of my work shirt was stained with vomit. I almost wanted to laugh, but I was too shaken to do anything but stare blankly at the storefront. I saw the small painted sign with an arrow reading LOADING BAY and followed a cramped alleyway down to the back of the shop, where a large garage bay with several doors beckoned.

At the sound of my engine, a bristly old man in flannel and jeans appeared from a doorway. I could hear him speaking to me as I stepped down from the cab.

"Howdy, stranger! I wasn't expecting you for another hour, you must've..." he began, but his voice trailed off as he took in the sorry sight of me. "Uh...Son, are you okay?" he asked with genuine concern. For a moment, I only looked at him, he looking like so many other salty old Native Americans I'd seen across the country, with a beer belly and long hair kept back in a messy horse tail. How could I tell this man that I had just witnessed an event that happened years ago, an event I had been blessedly spared from witnessing thanks to my extreme inebriation.

"I...I... Uh. Just, tell me which bay to pull into. I... ate some bad food at a truck stop. Didn't want to be late," I said, the only thing I could think to say. Even in my traumatized state, with the abhorrent site of a child's internal organs splayed out on asphalt burned into my memories, the old autopilot kicked in, forcing me through the motions of my job even if I couldn't think straight. But before I could get back in the cab, the man grabbed me, and forced me to look into his eyes.

"Oh, Jesus. Did you take 51 all the way out here?" he asked. I blinked, only looking at him. He shook me, trying to get me to snap out of it.

"Yes," I said. The man sighed, shaking his head. He muttered something in Navajo and then walked off, leaving me to stand there, confused. He returned a few minutes later, a plain gray t-shirt in his hands.

"Here, change into this. Are you…full-blooded?" he asked, handing the shirt to me. At first, I didn't understand the question, then shook my head no.

"I see. Well, you must have some very powerful ancestors then, or a heavy burden in your heart. The Chiwaa'e does not bother with white men or those not native to the ground here. I can tell he's paid you a visit. Pull your truck into bay four, and then go get some sleep in your cab. I got a skeleton crew here to unload everything." I obeyed, backing the trailer in, and then lying in the claustrophobic confines of my sleeper cab, trying to sleep but only reliving the hellish visions I was granted. It almost felt like going through withdrawal all over again. The pain, the guilt. At some point, with predawn light coming through the windshield, the man reappeared.

"Here, you're going to need this," he said, producing what I realized was a dream catcher, a real handmade one, not the aesthetic plastic webbed kind you saw in desert truck stops. Then he handed me a piece of paper with directions written on it.

"This is an alternate route, you'll take I-70 up through Colorado. It'll add some hours to the return trip, but I don't think you could survive another run-in with the Chiwaa'e. If you have any practicing shamans in your family, I highly advise you seek their counsel upon your return. Tell them what happened. You have a piece of it in you now, and it will poison you for as long as you have it."

AFTER RELAYING my harrowing tale to Johnathan upon my delayed journey home, he explained the demonic spirit I had run into, a lesser-known elemental demon that, unlike the wendigo, preyed upon those whose souls seek redemption instead of damnation. I wanted to think it was all one bad dream, sleep deprivation, something, but the renewal of my anxiety attacks and alcohol cravings returning ten-fold told me that

I was indeed poisoned. Since writing this, which Johnathan encouraged as a way of purging the Chiwaa'e's presence in my soul, I have dosed peyote six times, done so in a sanctioned sweat lodge, under the supervision of men much wiser and nobler than I, their mystic knowledge and words used to excise the malingering presence in my soul.

Along with abandoning any sort of vehicular transport, I have joined Johnathan on the path of returning to my heritage, of spiritualism. With each profound trip brought on by the sacred cacti, I feel myself slowly returning to normal, and closer to my ancestors. Yet at night, when I lay awake in bed, I still cannot purge from memory those visions I saw out in the desert. I understand this is my punishment, my repentance for my crimes. But this knowledge doesn't lessen the suffering, the agony. I suppose it never will.

10

THE CONVERSION

I WAS TOLD that honeymoons are supposed to be a time of joyous celebration. A defining moment, the beginning of a new chapter. I was told these things were supposed to be happy. Not that ours was bad, necessarily. Linda and I didn't fight, our plans weren't ruined, we still had a good time, and I was genuinely enjoying myself, up until the night she showed me her discovery anyway. Yet that week in the Sierras changed my wife, and not in the self-actualized, positive manner the self-help books talk about.

It was her idea, which surprised me because Linda is not the outdoorsy type of person at all. In the four years prior that we were together, she almost always chose entertainment that involved climate control, refrigerated beverages and catered food. So, when she told me she wanted to spend a week camping up in a small patch of land her grandfather owned in the Sierras as a post-nuptial celebration, I didn't know what to say. Of all the family get-togethers I had attended, I never heard about her family owning any land, but three months prior to our wedding, she informed me her grandfather, who had been deceased for ten years, owned a few acres of land just outside of Lone Pine Creek. She showed me grainy pictures of the farmstead they had out there, and the breathtaking views of Mount

Whitney and Lone Pine Peak in the distance. When I asked what spurred her sudden urge to visit the place, which had sat unattended since his death, she informed me that her mother planned on auctioning off the land next year, and she wanted to go out there one last time and indulge in the beauty of her family's rugged homestead with her bride-to-be. It sounded good to me.

Despite living in California all my life, I had shamefully never ventured east, to take in the gorgeous scenery that was only three hours away from my apartment in Los Angeles. I personally had ideas of taking a cruise in the Mediterranean, or perhaps Hawaii. But we had a reputation to uphold as the non-conventional progressive couple, and I could tell Linda was anxious to go out there. So I acquiesced, and on top of all the other wedding-planning induced stress, I went about spending a small fortune at the sporting goods store a week prior to our trip, getting everything I could conceivably think of that we would need for a week of roughing it in the woods.

It was two hours of driving up roughly cut mountain gravel roads to get to the spot, and I was too preoccupied by keeping the Subaru from careening off the cliffsides to take in much of the splendid beauty surrounding us. It wasn't until we came to the top of a rounded dome hill, which granted us with a spectacular view of the valley below, that I realized why Linda was so excited to come out here.

The intense shades of green, brown and blue that dazzled my eyes was almost overwhelming as I took in the waves of pine tree-covered hillsides, blankets of grassy prairie hills and wild wheat that rippled in the wind like an endless sea of indigenous flora, the two blue tear drops of lakes that glistened with clean, clear water down below. Despite the disturbing phenomena I witnessed in this picturesque chunk of my home state, I could still go there today and appreciate the raw, powerful beauty of those wild lands, which was such an utter antithesis to the hues of gray and black filth that comprised Los Angeles's pallet. I didn't realize how accustomed I'd grown to the smog and buildings and the chaos of the city. I forgot such beauty could exist out here.

As I type this, I vividly remember one of the last normal moments me and Linda had together, and Christ, it was such a beautiful moment. We sat there, on the hood of the car, holding each other in silence and taking in the landscape, totally enrapt in each other's company. I remember when she looked me straight in the eyes, and said "Michelle, I can't tell you how good it feels to have two of the most beautiful things in the world right here in front me." What I would give to go back to the moment, to freeze it, cherish it, to simply take in the view, and then get back into the car and go home.

Instead, I drove a little farther up to the small field, and parked by the overgrown run-down cabin that served as the remnants of the Taylor homestead. After several hours of floundering with tent setup and figuring out how to work the portable stove, we decided to do some exploring. Linda was an avid swimmer, and I really wanted a chance to use the fishing rod I bought on a whim during my outdoorsman splurge, so we decided to set a path for the nearest of the two lakes. I thought the trip was going to be rough, as it appeared we were going to have to go through a dense tree line and half mile of prairie to get to it.

Except that wasn't the case. Linda managed to find a cleanly cut trail that led straight to the lake. This was when I started to get the first tinges of concern, as Linda had told me no one ever came up to this area of the mountains, there were no state sanctioned park trails that came anywhere near here, nor any farms or fire roads. Yet she didn't seem too concerned about this random path materializing before us, and I didn't want to spoil the mood, so I kept my mouth shut.

The lake itself was beautiful, the water breath takingly cold as we plunged in. We spent hours there swimming, and eventually, I tried my hand at fishing, where I eventually caught a nice-sized trout. By the time we decided to head back, the sun was about to set.

On our way back, we noticed there was a secondary trail that branched off to our right, which led up a hillside and into a deeper, more dense section of the woods. My sense of unease grew, as I was quite positive this opening was not there before, and for a moment I thought perhaps we had taken a different route back to camp, but I could clearly see the glint of the Subaru's paint job reflecting off the setting sun high above. We were on the right track.

Linda was feeling exceptionally energetic after our dip in the brisk, refreshing water, and wanted to follow the trail to see where it went. I did not. That opening seemed especially foreboding to me, as the overhanging tree line grew much denser on that path, making it darker, more uninviting, like a corrupt portal to some unwelcome destination that was sequestered away in all this postcard beauty.

But again, I did not want to ruin the moment. I mentioned the very real danger of mountain lions or the lone black bear, but Linda wouldn't have it. She plunged ahead, with reluctance I followed her.

We had only made it about thirty yards in before she stopped abruptly. She was staring down at something. I walked up and saw that she was looking at what appeared to be a small configuration of rocks. They were rounded pink stones the size of silver dollars that were arranged to form a perfect circle, and in the center of this circle was a large reflective obsidian stone that had some kind of engraving on it. This was clearly of human design, and for some reason this realization made me feel vulnerable, made me realize just how out of our element we were in this place, just two city-slicking women out in the middle of the wilderness. Twilight was upon us now, the walk here taking longer than I expected, my sense of time was all messed up. I shined the light farther down the trail as something caught my eye, and I saw that there was another rock configuration another thirty yards down trail, the center obsidian stone glinting off the flashlight beam.

"What the hell?" Linda said, anger in her voice as she went to investigate. She was obviously livid, thinking that some weirdos had been trespassing on her family's property, and she insisted we follow the rock trail. But I pointed out the fact that the trail seemed to go higher up into the beginnings of the mountain range ahead, the climb looked steep, and it was getting darker by the minute. With much reluctance on her part, we headed back to camp, where we consumed between us one of the bottles of Chateau Morgaux that her father had gotten us as a wedding present, and proceeded to crawl into our tent and consummate our wedding vows.

At some point in the night, I awoke, my body sore, head pounding from the wine hangover, and realized Linda was no longer in the tent. The tent flap was open, and I assumed she was using the bathroom. But ten minutes went by, fifteen, and she still had not returned. I started to worry, and went outside to look around, calling her name. When I realized she was not in the immediate vicinity, I panicked. I ran down towards the trail, as that was my first instinct, and saw a fleeting figure in the glow of my flashlight beam. It was Linda. I called her name and ran after her, but she ran ahead heedlessly. For a moment, I lost sight of her, and then I rounded a curve in the trail and saw her standing perhaps fifty feet ahead. She was completely naked, her pale skin shimmering brilliantly in the harsh beam of light, her feet dirty and covered in mud. I called her name, told her to stop fucking around, that this wasn't funny.

Then I remember vividly how she turned back towards me, a blank look on her face, making a come hither gesture with her right hand.

"I have something to show you," she said in a sultry, dreamlike voice, then bolted off to the right, towards the trail with the rock piles. I assumed she was still drunk, perhaps wanting to go for a kinky dip in the lake. I moaned and sprinted after her, thinking of the ass chewing I was going to give her, not thinking about the fact that Linda was left handed, that she had *always* made that inviting sensual gesture that precluded our love making with her left hand. I would realize this later, when she began to show other spontaneous, un-Linda like behaviors. But by then it was too late.

I ran after her, barely able to keep up as she bounded through the increasingly rugged trail, which went up at a steep angle and was stunted with rocks, tree roots, and those horrible rock formations, which were present at every thirty yards, as relentless and consistent as divider lines on the highway. I kept stumbling, falling, my flat top shoes betraying me with every other step, yet Linda, who had never shown a knack for coordination or athletic prowess, seemed to be floating along effortlessly, and at that point I realized something was truly not right here.

After what seemed like an eternal mile of sprinting and falling, my knees and hands raw and bloody, I almost ran into my love as I reached the summit of the never-ending hillside, and saw her as she stood transfixed, gazing longingly at the strangely terrible sight before us. She pointed ahead.

"It's so beautiful, what's on the other side," she said in reverent awe. I followed the direction of her finger to a small meadow that was recessed into the side of the mountain, about half the size of a football field. Tucked away in this little plateau was a small, perfectly round pond which had those familiar black rocks lining the bank.

"What the hell, Linda? What are you talking about?" I asked, but she ignored my tantrum and took my flashlight from me. She shined it into the pond, and I stopped my complaining as I saw that the perfectly clear water soon faded to black. I stood, looking confused, before realizing this blackness indicated abyssal depths, and that this pond was actually the mouth to some sort of submerged cavern that crawled away inside the large mountain surrounding us. But as I looked deeper, I saw something moving in the water, a faint hint of life far down in the depths.

"You… went in there?" I asked, grabbing Linda's arm, trying to get her to edge away from the cavern as I got an overwhelming feeling that this benign body of water had the intent to swallow us whole. That's when I felt her wet, cool flesh.

"Yes, Michelle, I went down, *in there*. God, it's so beautiful. You wouldn't believe it. Come with me. See for yourself. Words can't describe what's down there. It will change your life," she said, her voice slow and rhythmic, and that's when I noticed her pupils, dilated so much you could barely see either iris, as if she were peaking off a few hits of Molly.

"No baby, let's go back to camp. You need to lie down. I think someone had a little too much wine," I said, but my gaze kept coming back to the pond. There were colors swirling in the water now, obscuring the depths. They were such beautiful colors. I felt myself being pulled to the glassy surface like a magnet to metal. Summoning all my will power, I ripped my gaze away from the water, forcing myself to start walking towards camp, dragging a dazed Linda with me.

THE REST of the vacation was somewhat uneventful, except for the subtle aberrations in Linda's behavior. I noticed my wife slowly transforming in benign, but disturbing ways. I had caught a few brook trout in the lake over the week, and I volunteered to clean them and cook them, to make our outdoor experience more authentic. Linda, usually a squeamish person with no prior experience in cleaning or dressing animals, took over in that duty, gutting and cleaning the trout with alarming efficiency, and then began eating her filet almost raw with savage delight, barely giving the propane grill enough time to sear the flesh. She was much more quiet, introverted, and prone to long periods of almost catatonic contemplation as she sat on the edge of the clearing, staring off in the direction of the trail, and that goddamn meadow. When I asked her what was wrong, what had happened to her, why she was obsessed with that goddamn pond, she would turn to me, those eyes huge and glassy.

"I just want you to see what I saw. The beauty. There was… so much of it."

Her speech changed too. She always had the dialect and accent of a true blood Angelesan, but over the course of that week, her colloquialisms changed, her accent taking on some subtle stunted nature, as if she was slowly losing her comprehension of the English language. The love making was much rougher, Linda's normal silky moans of pleasure and languid demeanor turned into a primal, grunting assertiveness that I'd never heard her make, even during the early infatuation period of our relationship. She was much more prone to biting and choking during intercourse too, something I didn't exactly mind, but her carnal appetite was so intense and out of character that I, a woman of healthy libido, had a hard time keeping up with her. She was insatiable.

Along with these behavioral changes, I noted that every night, I was awoken very early in the morning by her return, but never her departure. Every time, she came back wet, and naked. I thought about asking her where she went during those nights, if she went back to that little pond, that little portal to her oblivion, where she said beauty beyond this world was to be witnessed. But instead I laid silently, pretending not to be awake, wondering what could possibly be down there, and who had put those stones there. Who had led my wife to be changed? Had someone orchestrated the fate of an innocent woman to be invaded by some eldritch force?

Then there was the most important question of all. The one that haunted me for days afterwards:

What was on the other side of the water?

IT'S BEEN two weeks since we got back. I prayed that perhaps Linda's abnormal behavior was a symptom of our surroundings, and that she would be back to normal in the concrete jungle of LA. But instead her "condition", that's the only thing I can think to call it, has only deteriorated. I have begun cataloging all of her changes, from her now short temper to her sudden preference for right handedness. The way she sometimes gets up in the middle of the night, and stands at the foot of our bed, staring and looking up at the ceiling for over an hour, stock still, and then coming back to bed without a word. She mutters in her sleep, speaking in a harsh guttural language I do not understand. I inquired of her coworkers to see if they had noticed anything bizarre as well, and to my horror, they had.

Linda is a graphic designer, and according to the office, people who come by her workstation note with some concern that she has been caught creating disturbing images of hideous creatures emerging from some abstract primordial waterway, or perhaps it is a portal;

they could not tell. I'm told that she has not completed any of her assigned work orders, and her desk is covered in small post-it notes, on these are what appear to be long ramblings in a mixture of English and some unknown language. Her boss wants her to see a therapist or something, insisting that perhaps work stress is causing her to have a breakdown.

How do I tell them that my wife is slowly being taken away from me? That the person known as Linda Taylor is now, slowly, being inhabited by some force or being that she absorbed while venturing into a flooded cavern in the Sierra foothills?

Today she announced she was taking two weeks off of work and going back out there. She insists I come. She says she has things to show me, to help me understand. It is the only way she can continue to be married to me.

God, I love her so much. I can't stand the thought of her being taken away from me. She says if I go down there with her, that I will understand, and that things will go back to normal. The thought of going into that small abyss frightens me to no end. The thought of what I might experience to cause me to change like her makes my hands shake as I type this. Yet the idea of having to live the rest of my life without her, or with some alien façade of her, makes me even more afraid. They say love makes us blind, and I guess that's true.

I'VE BEEN THINKING. I've decided that I would rather change and continue a harmonious existence with my love, than eek out an existence in this confusing, horrible world alone.

We go back tomorrow.

11

RIENE DE L'ENFER (THE QUEEN OF HELL)

Shaun piloted the air boat carefully, the swamp he once knew so well transformed into a strange water-logged hellscape, all his typical land markings gone, washed away by Hurricane Selma. He wouldn't admit he was lost—he was a fifth generation Ladeur—he knew these swamps, or thought he did. But it was nighttime, the hurricane had leveled and destroyed many of the old shotgun shacks perched along the main channels, and it had been over a month since he'd last been back here. His memory was admittedly distorted after laying low from the bank robbery he'd done up in Alexandria. He'd done a lot of drinking and smack-slamming at his buddy Aaron's house during that time. He meant to make clean off with the $30k, but had to shoot two bank security guards who decided to play hero that day and because of that, the great state of Louisiana would *very* much like to see him ride ol' sparky.

So, being the swamp rat he was, he'd decided to hide twenty-five grand of the heist money in the last place anyone would look, that place being one of the nastiest, most isolated bayous Louisiana had to offer. He turned right, the spotlight fixed to the air boat swiveling with him as he cautiously perused through a maze of cypress trees, wincing as he passed through messy waterlogged spider webs, the bloated orb weavers scurrying for safety as he barreled through their homes.

"Come on, where the fuck are you?" Shaun growled, trying to peer through the fog that further obscured his vision, hiding the many dangers that lurked out here. He thought he'd seen some structure over here from the main channel, and assumed it was the old shack he'd found while on the run, the one he'd held up in for four days, praying the state police would assume he'd fled by highway and not bother with these nasty backwaters, a gamble that paid off.

His plan was to stash the money at the shack, which looked to have belonged to an old swamp hermit, and lay low there until the heat was off. But then hurricane Selma changed his plans and he'd barely gotten out of the swamp alive. Luckily the police were so preoccupied with evacuations that he was able to hide out in an old trap house he used to deal out of just outside of Holloway. So here he was, back in the swamp, the blood of the man whose airboat he'd hijacked gathering a miasma of flies and mosquitos as it dried on the hull. *Just get the money, and get the hell out of dodge. Then you can buy all the dope your heart desires.*

"WHAT IN HOLY HELL," Shaun muttered as he came through a particularly nasty patch of drift wood and smashed trees, to a clearing that revealed the bloated hull of an honest to god Tom Sawyer era steamer. It was a triple decker by the looks of it, the rusted smokestacks poking crookedly out from the top. He was so transfixed on the bewildering site that he nearly jumped out of his skin when he heard the huge splash of an agitated gator that he'd bumped with the bottom of his boat. He watched it swim away just under the surface of the water, and noticed it's body glowed blood red.

He took another snort of white china from the bullet necklace he kept around his neck, wondering if it was possible for smack to make you hallucinate. He cursed as the comforting rush of euphoria he expected did not come. He froze with the bullet halfway to his nose for another whiff when he thought he heard voices, and immediately cut the engine, the fan blades whirring to a stop.

He paused to listen, expecting to hear the chorus of swamp fauna singing to him, the crickets, the cicadas, the incessant whine of mosquito wings. But he realized then as he floated nearer the boat that the swamp was completely silent, as if he were in a vacuum, the swamp itself holding its breath, waiting to explode at any moment. Then he heard it again.

"Ladeur," came a voice that sounded as old as time itself. A chill went through Shaun just then, and he had to wonder if that four-day bender he was coming down from had scrambled his brains a bit.

"Hello? Come out goddammit!" He called out, his voice immediately swallowed by the heavy atmosphere. He found that odd, as usually a voice echoed off the water, *swamp acoustics* his grandfather called it.

"Come see," came the voice, rusty like an old screen door, the Cajun patois was thick, the old French flavoring shaping the vowels in that strange nasally way. He tried to start up the airboat again, but the outboard powering the fan turned, spinning the blades momentarily, before unceremoniously coughing to a stop.

"The fuck?" Shaun said, trying to turn the key again. Nothing. He whirled suddenly as he heard the massive wooden hull give a miserable creak of rotten wood. He looked up to see that he was level with the boarding platform on the starboard side, a rusted step-up leading to the main deck. As soon as his hand made contact with the ship, a brilliant crimson glow blossomed from inside the boat, washing him in brilliant red radiance. Shaun stared mesmerized, not realizing he'd begun climbing up onto the main deck until the loud shriek of rotten planks underfoot shocked him out of his daze.

He tried to turn back and get on the boat, half thinking he'd paddle his damn way out of here if he had to, but something kept him planted to the boat. It felt like someone had cranked a knob on Earth's gravity up to eleven, each step feeling heavy and labored. He found himself entering the boiler room, a miasma of wood rot and stagnant flood water almost making him gag. His nausea vanished when he saw the abhorrent decorations that lined the interior of the room. The hunk of charred metal that was once the boiler was festooned with what looked like dream catchers made out of fish bones and bleeding muscle tissue.

Lining the walls were snake skins of a species he'd never seen before, their scaled skins a purest obsidian and streaked through with red. He suddenly had a thought then, a flashback to when he was just a child, riding in a canoe along the outer edges of the Kisatche River with Grampa as they catfished.

"There be bad things up in these woods," Grampa Ephraim had said. "People out there who still practice the old magic, craft those voodoo abominations, hide out in the swamp, doing God knows what with that devil's knowledge." Shaun had just thought his gramps was slipping. Ephraim did get Alzheimer's early on, rambled a lot about Haitian witches and swamp demons. "Swamp knows when someone shouldn't be there. It *lets* you exist, it *lets* you harvest the gators and the fish and the wood. You piss it or the people that call it home off though…God help you."

The old man's ramblings suddenly took on horrifying validation as Shaun walked further into the ship, the decorations becoming more terrible as he entered the main ballroom, where decaying corpses dressed in water-logged suits and dresses danced some abhorrent shuffling jig. The sound of their atrophied tendons and bones grinding together in a hellish cacophony made Shaun want to cover his ears and scream, but his hands had become two-hundred-pound sacks of numb, useless meat. He caught glimpses of skinless catfish nailed to the walls, still twitching and croaking for life. The skins of human bodies were tacked below this the way bear pelts were often proudly displayed. A wooden sign proclaiming the vessel's name was framed above the interior walkway of the hurricane deck. *Riene De L'enfer.* Shaun's knowledge of the old swamp creole was rusty, but he knew enough French from his traditionalist grandfather to decipher the plaque. *The Queen of Hell*

"Come see," came the voice, this time coming from everywhere at once, inside his own head. An invisible hand pulled him to the right, where he saw a stairwell that led down into the ship's bowels, the scarlet glow deepening.

"No," Shaun whimpered, terrified of the fact his body was not moving of its own volition anymore as he headed down the stairs, something driving him down into the depths, his hand touching the damp banister of rotten wood as he slowly descended. He came to the state rooms, which were inundated in water up to his knees. Despite the sweltering Louisiana summer outside, the water was ice cold, causing his manhood to shrivel up into his body. He saw shapes swimming about just under the water's surface as he walked down the hallway.

A shape floated nearby as he walked, and when he looked down he saw the familiar bloated face of a bank security guard, a chunk of his skull missing.

"Oh god," Shaun croaked, clutching at the bullet necklace. He fumbled the lead cap off and cried out as his trembling useless hands dropped it into the murk below. "Fuck!" He screamed and shot his hand down into the water, desperately needing a comforting snort. A bony vice locked on his wrist instead, pulling him down into the water. He tried to back away and pull his hand free, but this thing had the strength of Goliath behind it. Shaun was pulled under water, his eyes taking in the face of the other security guard he'd shot, his uniform peppered with holes from the buckshot, floating freely about a body whose flesh was as pale and sallow as a catfish belly.

"Come see," the man said, no air bubbles coming from his ruined, lipless mouth as he spoke, the voice clear in Shaun's head. He cried out, and foul silty swamp water filling his mouth, causing him to choke and splutter. Finally, the corpse let go, and Shaun shot up, coughing and gasping for air. Wanting to run up the stairs, up and out of this damned steamer and take his chance with the alligators, Shaun instead continued down the hallway, his head moving involuntarily from side to side as he glimpsed into the doorless rooms.

In the first room he found his mother, naked and lifeless on a bed, a trail of gore blossoming between her legs. His abusive alcoholic father stood by her, holding a tiny blood-covered Shaun in his arms.

"Aint nothing but a bastard, killed the only woman I ever loved. Should've been you that died," his old man said. In another room, Shaun spotted the corpse of a woman named Loretta Bailey, whom he'd raped and killed in a drunken rage, she being the only woman he'd ever been intimate with.

"Why'd you do me like that, baby?" she asked, her voice nothing but a rasp from atrophied vocal cords, wet sounds coming from the open wound in her throat where he'd sundered her jugular. Two more rooms loomed ahead.

In the next one he spotted all the animals he'd ever killed, legions of cats and dogs and his stepmother's chinchillas he'd stomped on for fun, back when his adolescent brain was beginning to bloom the synapses that would associate sadistic killing with orgasmic pleasure. Some abhorrent arcane energy powered their matted furry corpses, a cacophony of hisses and growls assailing him as he walked past.

He braced himself for the horrors of the last room, a large suite estate at the end of the hall. But there was nothing in this one, except the glassy surface of the water, undisturbed by his treading. He froze, looking down into it, confused by what he saw.

It was himself, Shaun, laid out in the hull of the air boat, the bullet chain necklace in his hands. The airboat floated in the middle of the swamp, early morning sun painting the scene in a crimson glow. A legion of flies buzzed around his head, landing on his cloudy open eyes, some tasting the white crust around his nostrils and dropping dead instantly.

Shaun understood then, with horrible clarity. His buddy had said this particular batch was some *real* good shit, cut with fentanyl, which was supposed to be some of the highest-grade doctor dope this side of the Mississippi. He remembered taking a few more extra snorts than usual after he'd iced the alligator hunter the boat belonged too, needing the energy for the task ahead.

That's why he had no memory of actually entering the swamp. It was why he just sort of showed up randomly in the mired hollow with the steamer. He was dead, had died in this mystical backwater that his grandfather had treated as a living, breathing, sentient entity. His soul was its to chew on and masticate, to punish and rape.

"Is this...Hell?" he asked the room aloud.

"Come see," the voice enticed him. A split second later the floor beneath him gave out, and Shaun Ladeur plunged down into the murky depths, being swallowed by the swamp into an obsidian gullet of eternal heat and suffering.

12

THE WHITE SUITS

SHE HAD BEEN WALKING for hours, sticking close to the bank, the nearby swollen brown river her compass. Every five minutes or so she cast furtive glances around, looking through the bare trees for any sign of movement. It had been weeks since she had last encountered anyone, neither white suit nor a lone immune scavenger such as herself. She felt very alone, isolated, but at the same time always on guard, like a prairie vole crossing the killing field of the hawk. She wished desperately to find someone such as herself, a friendly soul. But everyone she'd come across on her travels either meant her harm or wished to abduct her for unknown reasons. She spotted a group of kids once, close to her own age that she followed for a few miles, working up the courage to approach them. But the White Suits got to them first. So, she went on, doing her best to commit her parent's teachings to memory on her journey. *Keep your head low, Elle, and move lightly. Always assume someone is watching.*

It was approaching dusk when she finally decided to stop. She almost didn't want to, the walking and physical exertion keeping her warm, but she knew she'd have to find food and a place to settle in for the night soon. She knew she was close to the city, which made her nervous. Her father's voice came floating back to her like a welcome specter. *Stay away from major population centers. Places with the tall buildings and lots of glass, concrete. Those places aren't safe for young women, or any women for that matter.* But she had to cross through if she wanted to keep going south. Down south is where the enclave of survivors was, those like her, who supposedly would offer her sanctuary and safety from the White Suits.

She was on the barren outskirts of an old riverside oil refinery. She stuck to the patch of woods bordering the large rusting tanks and fences housing them. A long metal feeder tube propped up on high stilts jutted out over the water, its once straight and white frame oxidized and warped precariously, tilting hard to the right. Elle thought even a light breeze might be enough to topple it over into the swirling current. In the distance, she could see the buildings towering above the fading tree line. A huge scabrous curving structure could be seen off to the right, close to the river. It too took on a dangerous lean. Elle vaguely remembered when that structure was once beautiful, gleaming with its reflective metal panels bouncing off the sunlight. She even remembered riding atop it once in something called an elevator. But that was when she was just a toddler, before the sickness came. *The world outside is nothing like you remember it, Elle. You can't trust anyone.*

She tied her long black hair back with the twine she kept in her coat pocket, and hastily gathered driftwood from the silty bank, careful not to slide in the muddy patches towards the frigid water, although she'd have to get down there eventually to catch her food. The thought of cooking fish made her stomach rumble. She hoped she could catch a bass. She'd been eating carp for the last three months, and carp meat was always oily and metallic tasting. She longed for the white flakiness of a bass, or even a catfish, like her dad used to fry up. But the river would provide what it provided, and sometimes it didn't provide at all.

She had with her a backpack containing the insulated sleeping bag, the two lighters she scavenged from cars, two bottles of water, and the remaining half of an expired Hershey bar she had already nibbled on earlier that day. The chocolate was hard and a little bitter, but she ate it anyway. Fond memories of Halloween and candy filled her with each bite. Strapped to the outside of the pack was her folded up cast net and the collapsible fishing rod that used to be her father's. She took the backpack off and unstrapped the cast net from the bag. She hated net fishing in the winter, her already cold-stiffened hands aching in protest at the thought of getting wet, handling the cold net and the frigid slimy fish she'd have to cut up. She had no choice however, the contagion having wiped out most land-based game early on.

Once she had a decent bundle of wood together, she sighed, going down to the bank, walking carefully so as not to fall in. The river swirled and ran fast here, and she could see the occasional derelict barge or slowly sinking tugboat go floating past. After a few freezing casts with the net, she managed to pull in a decent sized catfish, her favorite.

"Yes!" she said quietly, her stomach growling at the prospect of food. She began to salivate as she ran back to her little campsite, the net held victoriously in her hand. She wanted to shout and jump and laugh, but stifled the urge, casting more furtive glances around as the growing shadows and darkening sky encroached. She kept an eight-inch skinning knife in her boot that she brought out, a knife that had seen the insides of two men by her hand, but was always rinsed clean with Mississippi grit. She went to work.

She ate quietly, huddled close to the humble fire, her back to the river. It was very cold now, her fingers and toes growing numb, her nose runny as she ate the last of the fish. At least her belly was full, and the annoying thing with the blood and the cramps that had been plaguing her the last couple of days had passed. She fought the urge to throw more wood on the fire, craving more warmth. Instead, she forced herself to put one small branch on at a time, keeping the fire low, not wanting to draw attention. She reluctantly went away from the fire to answer the call of nature before scurrying back and burrowing deep into her sleeping bag, inching as close to the blessed warmth as she could without setting herself ablaze.

She was on the verge of sleep, trying to think about the good memories she had with her family before the sickness came, when she heard it. The snap of a twig. *Crack.* Like a gunshot in the eternally silent night. Her eyes opened suddenly, all pleasant recollections of her life prior to the sickness evaporated. She blinked, trying to get herself adjusted to the night. The moon was half out, casting a weak glow through the trees. That's when she saw it, the figure, frozen in mid stride. A skinny, twig like silhouette with ratty clothes.

Every encounter she felt the same. Just like when the scavengers found their house, those crazed and cannibalistic survivors who had stormed the isolated cabin with guns blazing, her bleeding and wounded dad shoving her into the tunnel that led out to the river. A mixture of fear, adrenaline, and mild vertigo as the reality of having to fight for your life hit. She kept calm. He clearly was not a white suit, that's what was important. And he was alone. *Learn to choose when to fight and when to run, honey. Each one has its place.* She learned to do both well, her mother's calm but firm voice directing her as she taught Elle how to use the knife, becoming proficient with both hammer grip and the modified saber grip. She had the little .22 pistol in the bag with her as well, but she dared not use it on a scavenger. That was for the White Suits. Or for herself, if it came to that.

She lay there, totally still, waiting. When the interloper thought she was still asleep, he continued, carefully. Slow, deliberate steps. As they approached, she thought she could see a beard flowing out from the hooded head. A man. He approached her backpack, which was at the foot of her sleeping bag. She waited until he was only a foot away, crouched over to pick it up. That's when she erupted from the bag, knife darting forward in a quick flash. She felt it scrape off his ribs before sliding cleanly into his chest. He let out a wet gasp, before hammering her in the face with a bony elbow. She cried out, recoiling, but didn't let go of the knife, it sliding out of his body as she was flung back.

The man began crawling away from her, moaning, trying to speak.

"Just…wanted…food. Fuckin…bitch," he said between watery breaths. She stood there, wet knife in one hand, the other holding her throbbing nose. The man left a dark smear on the pale sandy shore as he tried to crawl away, a black stain in the pale gray of moon reflected earth. He crawled about fifty feet before he stopped, a death rattle escaping him. She quickly went down to the bank of the river, shivering as she thoroughly washed the blade in the freezing silty water. She came back to camp, blowing on the smoldering embers of the fire, cupping her hands around the small licks of warmth that trailed up from the ashes, and then crawled back into her bag, ignoring the dead man. *Things have changed, Elle. It's either you or them. It's always you or them. Remember that.*

SHE STUCK to the back alleys and close to walls. She walked quick. Her two-week journey so far had brought her through forests and the occasional strip of farmland, her parent's cabin intentionally far away from any metropolis. This new landscape of grey and brown, of manmade decay and depravity screamed at her senses as she navigated through the industrial ruins of East Saint Louis. She passed through large factories with broken windows, the walls covered in graffiti, some of which was colorful and almost beautiful. Others showcased ominous messages in a scrawling hand. THE RAPTURE IS HERE, THE SIN IS THE DISEASE, or DON'T TRUST THE CDC THERE IS NO CURE.

She thought she heard distant voices as she went on, as well as the thudding of shoes on concrete. Her own ratty shoes barely made a sound on the sidewalk, but she still felt ostentatious and vulnerable as she walked, the many black rectangles of factory windows on either side of her hiding potential spying eyes. In fact, she was so fixated on the windows, her head pointed up, vigilant eyes scanning all nooks and crannies, that she almost didn't see what was right in front of her. She had come to the end of an alley, where she came out to a potholed parking lot next to a street filled with empty cars.

She froze as she heard distant radio chatter. Electronic devices. No one would have access to powered things, except for the White Suits. She turned to run in the opposite direction, and when she did, she saw it. The humanoid figure that stood before her looked something like an astronaut from the science encyclopedias her father had showed her. He put his hands up in a gesture of amicability, and spoke through a speaker, the voice male and almost robotic.

"Ma'am, do not be afraid. We want to help you. Please, don't run," he said in a voice that was almost pleading, slowly taking a step forward. "We can help you." Elle turned to run back the way she had come, but saw two more of the figures in white neoprene suits and reflective face visors walking towards her. She saw one of them had a pistol like hers. "Ma'am, we have a safe place we can take you. There's dangerous people out here," he continued, his voice modulated but seeming sincere. She had only ever seen the White Suits from afar, while in hiding or on the computer screen at the cabin, before the grid went down. She hadn't expected the encounter to go like this. This man seemed nice. He seemed like a friendly.

"I wanna see your face. Take it off and explain who you are," she said, slowly reaching for the pistol.

"I can't. I'm not like you. The disease doesn't affect you. Don't you understand? We can help you, help *us*. You could save our species, young lady. That's what we're trying to do." Desperation was in his voice. He took another step closer. She stood, conflicted. She was about to speak again, when she heard a small popping sound, followed by what felt like an insect biting her neck. She gasped, taking the hand away from the pack and swatting her neck. Her hand pulled away, revealing not an insect but a dart. She didn't understand, but didn't have time to think. Her body suddenly felt like it weighed a ton, and she dropped the pack, collapsing to the ground.

She came into and out of consciousness a few times before coming awake fully. She was aware of bright, reflective surfaces. Of needles poking and prodding her. The faint mechanical chirp of medical equipment that she was hooked up to. Of murmured voices discussing things like gene farming and blood isotope levels. Faint episodes that weaved into and out of her memory.

When she was fully awake, coming to in a room with a white so dazzling it hurt her eyes, she realized how weak she was. She saw she was lying on a gurney, a sheet draped over her body, plastic tubes of various sizes and some filled with what looked like blood trailed from the side of the bed. She followed these with her eyes and saw the bizarre looking machines she was hooked up to. She stared in disbelief at the HD monitor on a wheeled stand next to the bed, displaying a squiggly line that jumped in time with her heart beat. She couldn't remember the last time she saw an illuminated screen. Other gizmos surrounded the funny looking screen, as well as several large clear bags hanging suspended from a hooked stand. She grabbed a corner of the white sheet, observing it for a moment before pulling back, marveling at its brightness, its cleanness. Then she whipped the sheet back, and gasped at what she saw.

She was totally naked, her skin gray and sallow, the veins standing out like purple worms in her flesh. She marveled at the thin, emaciated frame that was her body, which she had never fully glanced at in such harsh, honest light. Against the back of the room the white walls were interrupted by a large reflective mirror tinted a dark shade. Elle could see herself in the mirror. She looked like a skeleton with skin pulled tight over the frame. Her eyes were sunken and hollow, her hair thin and limp against her skull.

She saw the myriad of wires and tubes hooked up to her forearms and legs, the entry sights purplish and bruised where several puncture wounds clustered together. She reached to pull the first tube from her left arm.

"Please don't do that," a metallic sounding voice said. Elle flinched, looking around wildly. She grabbed the sheet again and covered her wasted body. She curled up into a ball, ripping off the sensor pads and wincing as she pulled needles out of her arms. A beeping sound emanated from the walls.

Part of the white wall slid away revealing a black rectangle, and two people in those awful white suits came in. One of them immediately went to her. Elle tried to strike out, but it made her head swim to do so. The anonymous White Suit blocked the blow easily, and pinned her down.

"Get the transfusions hooked up again, quick, before she goes into shock," he said through a suit intercom to the other one. But the other suit didn't move.

"Dave...are you sure about this? We've already killed so many others like her. We've isolated her genes over a hundred times so far. You know we aren't any closer to sequencing a —"

"I SAID HOOK HER UP GODDAMNIT!" the one named Dave screamed. When he looked back and saw the suit slowly backing away, towards the door, he screamed again. "SECURITY, GET ME A FUCKING RESEARCH TEAM THAT WILL ACTUALLY FOLLOW ORDERS." He began rudely shoving the needles back into her nearly collapsed veins.

"W...What...What are you doing?" she asked, the world starting to turn gray.

"Trying to save the rest of our asses. But you wouldn't understand the imperative, you're just a dumb fucking kid like the rest of them," he said, trying to straighten out her arm. When she stopped resisting, and went limp, he looked down at her with his reflective faceplate. Her eyes had rolled back, revealing the yellowed sclera. "Oh no... Oh no you fucking don't. Come back to me goddamnit!" he said, and began performing CPR on the lifeless body. "SECURITY!" he screamed again.

Two men came rushing into the room, but by the time they arrived, it was already too late. The man, in a fit of rage, upended the gurney, the corpse spilling onto the floor. Everyone froze, and after a brief moment of silence, he spoke to himself.

"Patient 450 is now expired. Time of death, twelve-oh-five PM, March third, 2025. Two years research. Still no vaccine." He watched as the two security personnel bagged the small body up. He followed them down the hall towards the morgue, and watched as the body bag was placed next to over a hundred other bags, all of them much too small to fit an adult.

He didn't know why so many children were immune to the virus. He also didn't understand why they couldn't replicate the RNA sequence for the antibodies needed for a vaccine. The sequence of the virus was too long, too complicated. He knew now what the governmental agencies of the world once suspected: It was a man-made virus, but where it came from, and why it was released upon the world were things that still eluded him. So many innocent lives lost trying to find an answer. He was numb to the site of the many small lumps of neoprene, telling himself the children would've died anyway in this world gone feral. He'd recently been in contact with the only other active labs left, one in Toronto and another in Seattle, the virologists there reporting the same thing: It was mostly children who were immune. They too had harvested their fair share of young lives in search of an answer.

That was the one good thing about working in the end of the world. No ethics board to report to, no political hand tying to hinder your research.

No one left to call you a monster for simply doing what needed to be done.

RICHARD BEAUCHAMP

Richard Beauchamp is a North American author of horror and dark fantasy. Since starting his literary journey in 2017, Richard's tales have appeared in countless anthologies, podcasts, and literary magazines, having written hundreds of short stories and a handful of novellas up to this point. He may or may not have a novel tucked away in there somewhere as well.

You can find his works published in various literary magazines and award-winning anthologies, including *Gehenna & Hinnom's* "2017 Year's Best Body Horror" anthology, *Pub518's* "Influence of the Moon" anthology (A pushcart prize finalist), *Dark Peninsula Press's* "Negative Space: An Anthology of Survival Horror", *The Other Stories Podcast*, and *Scare Street Publications* "Night Terrors" volumes 3-5.

When he isn't sequestered away in his office getting lost in hells of his own making, Richard can be found deep within the Ozark wilderness, camping, fishing and kayaking. He's also been known to moonlight as a record producer, touring musician and video game composer under the alias *Shadrick Beechem*.

ABOUT THE EDITOR / PUBLISHER

Dawn Shea is an author and half of the publishing team over at D&T Publishing. She lives with her family in Mississippi. Always an avid horror lover, she has moved forward with her dreams of writing and publishing those things she loves so much.

D&T Previously published material:
  ABC's of Terror
  After the Kool-Aid is Gone

Follow her author page on Amazon for all publications she is featured in.
  Follow D&T Publishing at the following locations:
  Website
  Facebook: Page / Group
  Or email us here: dandtpublishing20@gmail.com

Copyright © 2021 by D&T Publishing LLC All rights reserved. No part of this book may be reproduced in any form or by any electronic or mechanical means, including information storage and retrieval systems, without written permission from the author, except for the use of brief quotations in a book review. This is a work of fiction. Names, characters, places, and incidents are a product of the author's imagination. Locales and public names are sometimes used for atmospheric purposes. Any resemblance to actual people, living or dead, or to businesses, companies, events, institutions, or locales is completely coincidental.

Produced by D&T Publishing LLC

Black Tongue and Other Anomalies by Richard Beauchamp

Edited by Patrick C. Harrison III

Cover by Don Noble

Formatting by J.Z. Foster

Corinth, MS

Made in the USA
Monee, IL
06 April 2025